MUSE

MUSE

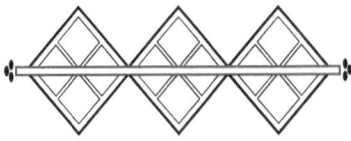

James Renner

CEMETERY DANCE PUBLICATIONS

Baltimore

❖ 2024 ❖

Cemetery Dance Publications
132B Industry Lane, Unit #7
Forest Hill, MD 21050
www.cemeterydance.com

The characters and events in this book are fictitious.
Any similarity to real persons, living or dead,
is coincidental and not intended by the author.

Trade Edition

ISBN: 978-1-58767-950-6

Cover Artwork and Design © 2019 by Elderlemon Design
Dust Jacket and Interior Design © 2019 by Desert Isle Design, LLC

For Brandy

Author's Note

THE following manuscript was transcribed from ten mini-cassette tapes that were recovered from the offices of Boston attorney William J. Latch following his disappearance on June 19, 2014. These tapes are part of the evidentiary record in the civil case of Latch V. Weymouth Life & Casualty and anyone can listen to them for free at the Suffolk Superior Courthouse. I have edited the tapes in a few places, mostly for clarification.

William J. Latch was declared dead by the State of Massachusetts in April 2015 after Magistrate Gavin FitzGerald reviewed these tapes, privately, in his chambers. Weymouth Life & Casualty was therein ordered to release Latch's survivor's benefits to his children.

Latch's body has never been found. His client, Michael Hadley, remains missing.

If you have any information about these unsolved cases, please contact Boston Police at 617-343-4240.

THIS is the last will and testament of Michael Hadley.

I, being of sound mind... Bill just go ahead and add all the legalese stuff.

As for what I got in the trailer down Ogunquit – just give it all to my niece, Amanda. Please donate my car to the Sisters of the Elms.

None of that's really important. Look, there's something else I need you to do for me buddy. I got myself in a hell of a pickle. By the time I realized it was a situation it was just too late.

What I'm about to tell you... all this started when I was working as a P.I. couple years after I ended my tenure at Portland P.D. I was living over in Veazie then.

For a minute I worked as a private investigator and there's one case in particular I need to tell you about. This is about that writer – one I mentioned when you come up last year and we went out for rolls down the harbor. It's that job I had to do for her but I didn't tell you everything about the case.

I had already worked for the kid's mother. Standard type of deal. She paid me to track down her old man who had run out on them. Dude was living in western Oregon. I gave the woman pictures that would help her in court and thought that was the last I'd hear of them.

Anyways about five months later I get a phone call and this time it's the woman's daughter. Younger one. Girl says she needs to meet with me, needs me to come over to their apartment in this shitty podunk town called Mechanic Falls. I go down there and they live in this shack ranch; it had a cement floor and everything.

So there was this woman and her two daughters, one being the writer I mentioned, then fourteen years old. The other was this tow-headed fuzzy duck. That one was a little older but she doesn't say boo the entire time. The writer – she's this kind of nerdy lookin lassie with the big coke bottle glasses and she wants to do the talking now, like she's in charge. I sat in a recliner in their big living room. They had one of those yarn paintings hanging on the wall the kind you buy at a garage sale for a thin dime – a butterfly. I remember they had all this weird North Country furniture that had seen three or four generations already. The kind of junk apple pickers load up on the backs of trucks and take from one town to the next.

I sit down and this kid she says, Mr. Hadley, we have another job for you and I says, What's that kid? And she looks at me very serious and says, Do you know H.P. Lovecraft?

Now you know me, I ain't read a book since fourth grade and I didn't know who the fuck H.P. Lovecraft was and didn't care. So she says, H.P. Lovecraft, the sci-fi writer. And I says, OK, sure kid. And she says, Well, I want you to steal this old box of his and we'll pay you twenty thousand dollars. And I didn't hear her right or at least I didn't think I heard her right so I ask her, What did you say? And she says I want you to steal an old box from H.P.'s estate and we can pay you three thousand for it.

And I ask the kid, What's in the box? And she says, does it matter? And I says, depends.

The girl looks at her mother and the mother just kind of shrugs her shoulders. And the way she did it kind of raised the hackles on the back of my neck. The girl, she looks back at me and says, I've wanted to be a writer all my life but it's not working. Nothing's coming out of the type-writer for me. Nothing like what Lovecraft could come up with on a whim. Lovecraft was *inspired*. Literally. What's in that box'll help me be a writer. It's at his lawyer's. And I want it.

I told her the thing that inspires writers is a fifth of bourbon and you could buy one of those for fifty-twice. But the kid couldn't be talked out of it. I figured what she was after was some lost manuscript or something. Something she could pass off as her own to get started.

Okay, I says, let me get this straight: what you want is some box that's still locked up somewhere in a lawyer's office. Is that it? How do you know this box even exists?

I've seen it, the kid says. I've seen it in a picture. Here, right here.

Now the girl takes out this I don't know – a large coffee table book – and inside are pictures of famous American authors. Jag-off writers with jag-off names I'd never heard of – Somewhere in the middle was this guy H.P. Lovecraft. He was this guy, this ugly looking dude with a long, horse-like face. Just looking at him made my skin crawl. Anyways the girl points to the bottom left corner of the picture and there right behind where Lovecraft was standing was this great oaken desk. And in the shadow of the desk on the floor was what looked like... well, it looked like one of those pirate's chests you see in some sort of Disney World ride or sideshow carnival. This old, crusty looking chest. It had one of those skeleton key locks in front.

Well? the girl says.

Well what?

Well don't you see?

It's a movie prop, kid. The picture was staged. It's supposed to make you feel creepy.

No, she says like I offended her. It's no prop.

And this time she brought out another book and this book was even older. It wasn't a picture book. It was one of those leather-covered books you find in the back basement of some county library. Something the library forgot seventy years ago. Just covered in a layer dust. It had the type of pale leather that looked like human skin. The kind we found in that file office at Dachau. The girl opens the book, fingers through some pages and comes to a chapter on ancient Greek mythology and shows me a woodcut carving, something they dug up in Pompeii or Athens or some shit. A picture of a… I don't know – some kind of goat creature. Like a half man – half goat. You know the kind with the human body and goat feet? Well it was one of those things and it was playing at this three-pronged pipe and sitting right next to it was this pirate chest looked just like the one from the Lovecraft picture.

What the hell is this? I ask.

It's a woodcut carving from Ancient Greece, the girl says.

All right. Tell me somethin I don't know.

It's the *same* box.

I looked at her sister who was sitting all quiet over by their mother. They both had this look of well I don't know, you'd call it *earnestness* I guess. This girl was obviously a most convincing storyteller in her own right even without whatever might be in Lovecraft's box. This hub cap had somehow convinced her family that this fairytale was true. And that was kind of frightening.

What do you really think is in this box? I ask the girl.

It's a secret, she says.

Well let's just lay it all on the table, I says. You want to pay me three grand, enough bread might I remind you that could put you into a better house than the one you're living in now, something without cement floors… To break into the office of H.P. Lovecraft's lawyer and steal a treasure chest prop that probably holds nothing more than some old sweaters and bring it back to you so you can open it and realize you're completely out to lunch?

The girl sighs and it was kind of off-putting, because it was a sigh of an old man. Like somebody that at least thought that they were smarter than I was. For a minute I wanted to punch her right in the face.

Look, the girl says. I guess I really don't care what you believe and what you don't believe but yes that's just about the sum of it. You go and steal us that box and bring it back here and we'll give you three thousand dollars.

♦ ♦ ♦

I wish I could tell you the girl's request was the strangest one I ever heard of but work in a city like Portland for a spell and you hear some pretty far out things. There was this one dude – big businessman in town worked at the hospital selling I don't know prescriptions or x-ray machines or something. Can't remember now. He wanted me to trail his mistress. He was concerned his mistress was stepping out on him. I followed her a whole damn week and she wasn't cheating on him. She was just going to the A & P. She'd go there every fucking night, sometimes she wouldn't even buy nothing. I'd follow her into the store and she'd just mope around looking at squash. Anyways the guy he paid me two grand for that job. Trailing his mistress making sure she wasn't cheating on him. Some people have too much money they don't know what to do with it.

Some kid and her family want to waste three thousand for a suitcase full of sweaters, fine. Except thinking back on it, it's one of those deals you hear about in books sometimes – a deal with the devil. Nowhere in life can you get three thousand easy. Not then, not now.

It was a long trip back to Veazie. At the time I was driving this wicked wood-paneled El Camino I'd hopped up with a bent eight. I remember that trip home listening to the AM stations over tinny speakers driving through the mountains. The whole thing just gave me the willies.

A week later, the telegram came. The slip was waiting for me on the floor of my apartment. You know those old telegrams, the yellow squares, little tissue paper they used to print them on – straight from Western Union. It was short. It was from the girl. Money is in escrow, she wrote and she gave me the name of a bank manager in Portland to contact. I checked the next day and sure enough there's fifteen hundred large sittin in there. Fifteen up front and fifteen on the back end.

Think it was then I realized for the first time that this was really happening and I was really going to do this.

But except for a name and a picture I didn't know dick about this H.P. Lovecraft fella. I needed background. What I really needed was a brainiac. I knew right away I ought to call Gil Holcomb.

Gil Holcomb knew more about books than anybody I ever met. Knew almost as much about books as he knew about buggering kids. Gil was this professor of English at the U-of-Maine, Orono. In his spare time he was a scoutmaster for the local Boy Scout troop. Anyways he took a handful of kids to Big Indian Mountain summer of 58 and when they come back one of the kids accused ol' Gil of some pretty lewd things. Said he was making the boys sit at the side of the tent and rub their socked feet on his crotch. Wouldn't think I hung around with a guy like that, huh? Well Gil and I both played the same gentlemen's poker game over at Doc McKaskel's house so Gil come to me when he got into that spot of trouble and I helped him. He was a bit of a fream but harmless. That's what I told myself.

Gil came to my office out in Veazie when that bit with the scout happened. Kid's got it all wrong, he says. Yes his foot touched my crotch but it was an accident.

Look Gil, I says to him. I really don't need to hear any of this.

But it's important to me that you believe me.

I believe you Gil. Now why do you need my help?

It's the Board, he says. They're going to take away my pension.

Shouldn't you be more concerned about criminal charges? I says.

No, no there's not going to be anything like that, he explains. I spoke to the boy's father and he understands. He called it a moment of weakness. He's a real good Christian fellow.

Then what business is it of the Boards'?

Ah… well, one of the other scouts. His old man is on the Board.

Did you bugger this kid too? I ask.

For a minute Gil goes blank and his eyes bug out of his head. And then he laughs. It was a prissy, silly laugh and he never did answer my question now that I think about it.

They're going to take away my pension, he says again. I need you to help me prove that this really couldn't have happened. That what the boy says isn't true.

It's just his word against yours, I point out. I mean what sort of proof could he have?

Gil goes quiet and looks up at me with Droopy Dog eyes I could tell was an act right away. Well, he says, I wrote him this letter.

What kind of letter?

It was just, you know, I was gassed and when I drink sometimes I like to sit down and write, stream of consciousness.

What exactly did you write in the letter to this boy?

Honestly, I don't... word for word? I don't remember word for word.

Clue me in, I says. What was the gist?

Well I know at some point... I don't remember writing this but the boy says...

For god sakes, man, make the words work.

I told him I loved him, he said.

I shake my head. And you would like to have that letter back?

Yes, says Gil. I would like to have that letter back very much.

A lot of times being a P.I. is going after insurance frauds, catching people breaking workers' comp, chasing lovers in the park. But sometimes being a P.I. is breaking into a kid's bedroom while the family's off to church and stealing a love letter that was written to him by his scoutmaster.

Gil lived in a tumbledown colonial on the south side of Orono over the railroad tracks in that section of town what used to be all prim till the Italians found it. He was packing his car when I pulled up. Tent, sleeping bags, a wide cast-ironed skillet for apple cobbler. He was dressed in his Class A uniform with a red flannel jacket tied at the waist the way paper-shakers wear lettermen jackets.

He looks up as I get out of the car. He's surprised to see me. Took him off guard. For a second I caught kind of a glimmer of what was inside the man. The monster behind the mask. Then his harmless fat-man smile washed over his face like a wave and took away the bad.

To what do I owe the pleasure? he says.

I smile and get a closer look and I follow him inside. He hands me a beer.

Gil, I says. I need to know everything you can tell me about this writer – H.P. Lovecraft.

He laughs. I never pegged you for a genre fiction man, he says.

No, no, no, it's not for me, it's for a new case I'm working.

Are you working for the Lovecraft estate? he says with kind of a look of hope.

No, it's a case I'm working for... it doesn't matter. Look, what do I need to know about this guy?

Well it sort of depends on what part of Lovecraft's history you're checking into. The man was a strange cat. You never read any of his stuff? Not even in college or high school English class?

No.

Well, the guy was an obsessive. He's what we call a "world-builder." He invented an entire mythology about a kind of under sea elder God thing called Cthulhu.

Cthulhu? I ask. Is that a real word?

Cthulhu, yes, well Lovecraft came up with it. C-t-h-u-l-u. It's just like when J.R.R Tolkien created the setting for *The Lord of the Rings* and *The Hobbit*. Lovecraft created his own worlds. But what he created was... darker.

Darker how?

Imagine a creature... say ten times the size of an African elephant. Black, oily skin, big barrel chest, large wide shoulders. A giant is what we're describing here. And it's got these two orbs for eyes and where its mouth should be are tentacles. Like on a squid. Pretty much something from your worst nightmares.

Who reads that fucking stuff? I ask.

Gil shrugs. Lovecraft was a good storyteller, he says. The way he presented his stories was new for the day. Since Edgar Allan Poe nobody had really ventured that far into out-and-out horror. In fact Poe was one of Lovecraft's chief inspirations. It goes a little further than that, actually. You see, Edgar Allan Poe only ever wrote one novel. It was called *The Narrative of Arthur Gordon Pym of Nantucket*. And it's all about this expedition that Pym takes to Antarctica – the South Pole— and Lovecraft if you look at his writings; everything goes back to Edgar Allan Poe. Specifically Poe's only novel *Pym*. Lovecraft imagined Cthulu as a creature, or rather this race of creatures, that once lived in Antarctica in this abandoned city called Leng.

It sounds like a bunch of bunk, I says.

Well you have to have a sense of the fantastic.

So this Lovecraft guy, he was devoted to Poe? What else do I need to know about this puff?

Lovecraft, there was this one other thing he was kind of well known for, says Gil.

What's that?

Well, he… in most of his stories he referred to a secret book. It was called the *Necronomicon*.

The *Necronomicon*? What's that?

The *Necronomicon* was supposedly a book written by this mad A-rab, Abdul Alhazred. This A-rab had once glimpsed the plains of Leng and the very sight had driven him insane. Basically, the book is the Satanic Bible.

So Lovecraft was a devil worshiper?

No, no that's not what I'm saying, says Gil, getting hot. That's not what I'm trying to say. Lovecraft was an academic. But… there is a bit of a mystery concerning his studies into Poe's methods. When Lovecraft was thirty-seven years old he got a bee in his bonnet you could say and he took off on an expedition to Antarctica. He believed Edgar Allan Poe had once taken a similar journey to a military outpost down there. Lovecraft was curious, as any scholar would be. He wanted to see if Poe had left anything behind.

What did he expect to find?

Nobody knows, says Gil. All we know for sure was that, in his day, Lovecraft knew more about Edgar Allan Poe than anyone. And if he thought Poe had been to the South Pole there's a good chance he had. Maybe Lovecraft found some documentation or artifact to prove it. What Poe was doing down there, what Lovecraft brought back... that's the real mystery. But when Lovecraft returned his writing got even stranger. Darker. And then three years later he died alone.

Gil gave me just enough to wonder if maybe this box the kid was paying me to steal might've come from Edgar Allan Poe. That it might actually be worth something, after all. Was this what Lovecraft had found on his expedition to the South Pole?

When Lovecraft died he didn't have no kids. No sons, no daughters, no nephews that he could will his stories to, so he donated the lot of his work to an estate handled by his friend and lawyer, Howard Antone.

Howard Antone was a professor of law at Miskatonic University, this stonewall school outside Salem, in Essex County. Old as fuck that place. Must be one of the oldest schools in the country. Got Antone's number from Arkham Press, the outfit that prints Lovecraft's stories. I remember the woman who answered the phone at Miskatonic was named Sarah. She was Antone's secretary. She had a lovely sounding lisp. Anyways, she put me right through to the professor.

Yes, who's this? he asks.

I pretended to be a Lovecraft scholar out of Syracuse working on a term paper. I was wondering, I says, if I came down to Miskatonic is the Lovecraft archive available for study? Artifacts and reports and you know, what's the world – ephemera?

Well, yes, says Antone. Most of Lovecraft's handwritten notes and rough drafts of all of his books are here including the rare serialized novel. Everything can be viewed on appointment.

What about the treasure chest?

Professor Antone didn't answer for what seemed like ten seconds and then in a tired voice says, What treasure chest?

You know, I says as if it were no big deal. The one that's in that picture when they did that big story on him in *Life* magazine?

Are you working for that little cunt from Maine? he snaps. That sudden change to such anger, it jolted me away from the phone for a second. It was like he was suddenly another person.

Uh, I'm not sure I know what you mean, I says.

Listen, if you're working for that snot-nosed bitch, tell her I'm not selling. Just like I told her a week ago. And the week before that. Nothing in Lovecraft's archives is for sale. And certainly not the ironwood chest. And with that he hangs up.

If there's one thing in this life I hate more than scoutmasters who diddle kids its elitist pricks who hang up on me. I went to my room and packed my suitcase, one of those leather ones beat up around the edges with stickers of all the places I had never been. I loaded in three shirts and enough underwear to get me through a week. On top of that I dumped a box of nine's and my sig sauer. I didn't have a P.I. license that worked in Massachusetts but I didn't need one. It wasn't like I was going down there to arrest anybody. I was going down to commit some old-fashioned larceny. Even a P.I. license can't get you out of that kind of trouble.

By eight o'clock the next morning I was grinding gravel. My El Camino rocketed down I-95, the new highway they'd built along the coast.

Miskatonic University was a bunch of buildings made of the biggest slabs of granite I ever seen like it was a school built up from ruins. Some forgotten city. And the walls were a different shade of gray than I seen before. The grounds gave me the creeps to tell you the truth. They had all this ivy growing over the rock and it kind of gave the buildings a green skin – made them look like they were living and breathing. Anyways the whole time I was there I felt like I was being watched.

Didn't take long to find Professor Antone's office. It was in Taylor Hall on the south end of campus, a newer building three stories tall. But even though it was new its walls were thick slabs of granite as if they'd hauled them out of the same quarry the ruins come from.

I did a loop de loop by his office round 2:30 that afternoon. Antone was inside. I could see the guy talking to that Sarah woman – who was as attractive as her voice suggested over the phone. One of those girls with size D cans, you know what I'm talking about – the perky kind. You used to call them sweater demons, I believe. I always liked that. Anyways Professor Antone was this real spindly guy with this bright white mustache and wire thin glasses and this bowtie. You know when I talked to him over the phone I knew damn well that when I got down there he'd be wearing a bowtie. Anyways this pencil neck stood over Sarah looking down her blouse really creeping the girl out. I kept walking. There was nothing to do. The guy wasn't going to talk to me and if he knew I was there he'd likely move what it was I was looking for. I was certain that Lovecraft's archives were inside that building, somewhere. Figured I'd come back later that evening after everyone gone home.

While I waited, I got a room at this motel off I-95. Real dive of a place called the Pink Flamingo as if there are any other goddamn types of fla- mingos, you know? Ever seen a blue flamingo? Just a real flophouse. One of those motels for the temporarily homeless: guys kicked out of doors by their old ladies. I saw this one room three doors down from me, there were two kids playing out on a sidewalk stoop blowing bubbles, drawing on the sidewalk. A real depressing type of place but it was cheap and clean and didn't nobody care who you were.

I dropped off my stuff and found a greasy spoon near campus, this place called Ike's Diner run by a lady named Rhea. Rhea was the rode- hard-and-put-away-wet type, cigarette hanging out of her mouth, ashing on your plates. When she walked me to my seat I caught her eye. Somehow

I knew that she had noticed me. Maybe she was the type liked thick men in leather coats because even way back then I was pushing two-fifty.

I was on my second Salisbury steak when she slid into my booth and chatted me up about the Clippers game. Then she told me about her two daughters and how her old man ditched them and left her to live at the Pink Flamingo till she got back on her feet. And sure enough after a beer and a couple Jackie-D's we were back at the motel doing the Watusi.

Craziest sex I ever had man. There was this moment right around when Jack Paar come on that I thought my dick broke in half and it got to the point where she was just sitting on top at me doing her thing and her eyes half glazed over and she started to drool. I'd never seen a woman drool during sex and it was most disturbing and it totally turned me on. I gotta tell you I don't know what the hell was wrong with her old man. If I'd had a woman rode me like that no way would I have kicked her down to the Flamingo. Anyways I had to send her along come two in the morning. I had work to do.

It was nearing four a.m. by the time I got back to Taylor Hall. Not much trouble getting in. I used a flower bomb to pop side door lock. Used a dim flashlight to find my way. Easy-peasy Japaneasy. Made my way to the professor's office. His inner office smelled hinky like some mixture of shoe polish and farts. Whatever it was I didn't like it.

The chest wasn't in his office but behind his desk I found another door, an unmarked door that opened into a small gallery of sorts. The place reminded me of a room inside a museum where you go and sit on a hard couch in the center and look at water lilies and shit. Except the walls here were covered in crazy stuff: weird necklaces, figurines, all kinds of strange tchotskes and I knew this was what was left of the life of H.P. Lovecraft. This was his stuff.

There were file cabinets along one wall. I scanned a couple. Full of tax forms and book contracts. Nothing that made any sense to me. I took another trip around the room. In one corner, atop a pedestal, was a taxidermied penguin. Half its shoulder was missing, exposing the wire frame underneath and it smelled like briny ocean water. That coulda been my imagination, I guess. In another corner, an odd tiara like from some beauty pageant rested on a purple velvet pillow under a lamp. But the tiara was misshaped, too oblong for a human head. Behind this was a picture of Lovecraft himself, that gaunt horse-ish face of his, that endless chin. In the photograph, Lovecraft was wrapped in a thick fur coat and he was standing on the brow of a ship and behind him was two giant icebergs and a glacier that marked the beginning of some land mass. Gil was right. Lovecraft really had made a trip to Antarctica before he died.

Found several other odd things in this room but the most bizarre was something I discovered under a glass dome like an aquarium or somesuch. It was a sort of mucousy thing – like a jellyfish – except it had no tentacles and it kind of hovered in what I believe was water except there were no bubbles coming off the creature. It just kind of did its jellyfish dance in there suspended in the middle of the water inside the glass. As I watched it seemed to take on many different shapes, some almost geometric, like organized shapes whose true names only mathematicians know. It felt to me… for a moment there it felt like I was a kid again and I had gone up to the stage during some kind of play and glimpsed behind the curtain to find a man changing out of an animal costume. Like I was seeing something I was never meant to see and which was far beyond the understanding of my mind.

Sometimes the most important thing you see is what you don't see. I realized something was missing from this room. There was a patch of wood discolored from the rest of the floor. Rectangle in size about one foot by a foot and a half, an outline of something that had once – recently in fact – rested there.

Me and the kid we'd managed to spook the professor after all. Don't know if it had been my phone call or whatever business he got from the girl. Something had made Antone nervous enough that he had taken the treasure box out of the archives. Guy like him, though... somebody who doesn't often think outside the box, I could guess where he took it.

Professor Antone was in the phonebook. Everybody's name and address was in the phonebook, in 1960. Remember that? No telemarketers. No one scared of rapists picking a random house and tracking you down in the middle of the night. Later that year we elected Kennedy. World still believed in good stuff. We still trusted each other. That changed quick.

Anyways Antone he lived in a ramshackle square house on the outskirts of town. Not a particularly nice neighborhood. I parked across the street after I was sure Antone had gone to work and then I walked to the door like I had business there. I knocked. Had to be sure no one was home during the day and it's a lucky thing I did. I could hear her move inside, like an elephant slowly standing and ambling toward the door. There was resignation in those giant steps. I could hear it.

Door opened an inch before it caught on the chain. Mrs. Antone was a plump woman about five feet tall round like an apple and her eyes were all buggy and red and watery like she'd been crying. Or maybe she was afflicted. She sniffles and looks up at me and says, Yes?

Hello, ma'am, I says. I put my hand through the space in the door. She shakes it meekly. I'm selling subscriptions to *Life* magazine, would you... She was already shaking her head no.

No, we're not interested in any more magazines right now. Thank you.

She starts to close the door and that's when I hear a familiar sound coming from within, a sound I'd hoped not to hear. It was the sound of a heavy collar clanking against itself. And footsteps, padded footsteps with an edge to them – sharpened claws on a hard wood floor. Just before she closes the door I catch a glimpse of the creature within. It's a full-grown

German Shepherd, exactly the type of dog burglars hate. German Shepherds are smart, smarter than some humans, I reckon. And German Shepherds are spiteful. That's why they call them *German* Shepherds. I had to rethink my plan.

I decided the situation called for a Bloomenthal. What's that? you may ask. Well, Larry Reginald Bloomenthal was this burglar I put away in '56. Guy was a career criminal and for the span of about three years he terrorized the residents of Portland, Maine, in a series of profitable burglaries. He broke in to some of the richest homes in town and never got caught. I was still a detective then. He had us stumped. We had no idea how he was sneaking in because all these rich people had guard dogs and the dogs never barked.

Then one day Bloomenthal, his luck run out and he was nearly mauled to death by a lawyer's Mastiff. Bloomenthal was all kinds of mangled and the EMT's had just arrived and were attending to him. We asked the lawyer how his dog caught the guy and he walked me over to the side of the house, where Bloomenthal's muscle bag was still sitting on the ground below an open window. Next to the bag was half of a steak except it didn't look like a regular steak. There were yellow blobs packed into the meat.

Benzos.

See, Bloomenthal was doping the dogs with diazepam. He'd drug em and then wait till they flopped over. Simple, but brilliant. Why didn't your Mastiff go for it? I ask the guy. She's a vegetarian, the lawyer says. Shit. Some people what they do with their pets is they try to make them people too.

I rode down to the five and dime and bought me a steak. I couldn't get Benzos but I did one better. Rhea had some Nembutal for her nerves. She gave me two for a fiver.

Went back to the professor's house round three in the morning. I get to the window and I bring out the jimmy but it wasn't even locked so I

JAMES RENNER - MUSE

pushed it open. It creaked a bit against the warped wood pane. I put my hand inside and kind of gently skittered at the wood on the other side of the window. I acted like a mouse making the sounds a mouse might make crawlin through the walls. Soon enough I heard the jingle-jangle of the chain that was the German Shepherd's collar.

The dog marches up to the window expecting a mouse and as soon as it gets a whiff of me its haunches bunch up and it makes a very low, soft growl. I toss in that steak I'd stuffed with the yellow jackets. The dog gives a short yip and then it starts to paw at the meat on the floor. It chomps at it and looks at me with wide eyes like it was thanking me. It had been a long time since this dog had had real fresh meat maybe never. Ten minutes later he was snoozin in the corner.

I shoe-horn myself into the window, not wasting any time. Getting my thick gut around the frame was a might tricky. I roll inside and pull my dim flashlight out and look around. I'm in a dining room off the kitchen, the living room to my left. Inside the living room is what appears to be some sort of workable space. A staircase led to a second floor but I didn't dare step on the steps unless I absolutely had to. Something told me Antone probably kept anything Lovecraft had touched as far away from his bedroom as possible. Everything in that dead writer's gallery behind Antone's office had left me feeling queasy. Wouldn't want any of it in my house.

There was a door beside the pantry that I knew right away must lead to a cellar. I open it up and sure enough it goes down into a dark basement. I know if I go down there, there's no escape route. If the chest is down there and they hear me while I'm gathering the box, I'm pretty much done for. But I have to, right?

I go down into the dark listening as hard as I can for any sound or movement from above that might give me a few seconds warning to scurry on up again and out the back door. But I don't hear nothin so I keep going.

It's one of those dark, cobwebby basements always smell like mildew no matter how much you dry them out. It has a dirt floor and rock walls that are easily fifty years older than the house above, part of some original structure long gone. I look around and find the hot water tank and boiler. I see something tucked away behind it. It's a rectangle covered in a white sheet and I notice the white blanket is still white even though the basement is covered in black mold and dust. I rip away the sheet and sure enough underneath is that dark box.

It's made of some heavy ancient wood. Some sort of hardwood, ironwood I think Antone said. It has brass rivets all around it, arranged in some sort of decorative pattern, and a giant lock set into the front. When I try the latch I'm not surprised to find it locked tight. No matter. Wasn't going to open it anyways, that's not what I was paid for. I was just the delivery man.

So I bend down and find the indentations along the sides that allow you to lift it. I pick it up. As I do I feel something shift inside the box as if the trunk is empty except for a soccer ball that has just enough room to roll around a bit. It hits the side with a thunk and then makes no further sound. The whole thing weighs roughly forty stones I'd say. And while that's not much for an average man to carry, my body had kind of gone to hell since I gave up my blues. I had to take it slow.

I turn to go up the stairs and that's when the overhead lights click on. I see their feet at the top of the stairs. Antone is dressed in his pajamas and no surprise there; he's definitely the type to wear flannel pajamas to bed. His wife stands beside him in a blue chamois, eyes puffy and red. She's done some more crying. Heard me cause she wasn't sleepin. I stand there for a beat with the box in my hands and just look back up at them.

I'm calling the police, Antone says and he turns back to the kitchen, making for the phone.

Wait, says his wife.

What is it Helen? he snaps.

I can't sleep, she says. I haven't slept a minute since you brought that thing home. I hear it singing. It sings to me all the time. Howard, let him take it.

This seemed to shock the professor a bit. As if it was not something he had considered before. But you could tell it was something that the woman had been considering. It was all she was thinking about by then I think. Getting rid of the box.

He looks back at his wife, then to me. He nods his head.

Yes, yes all right Helen, he whispers.

I stood there not really comprehending what was happening.

Well dummy, you coming up or what? says Antone.

I walk up the stairs carrying the box still expecting him to maybe push me down the steps or try to hurt me in some way and then lock the door on me until the police arrive.

Do you want some dough? I ask. I had sixty on me.

I don't want your fucking money, he says. Just get that goddamn thing out of my house and never come back.

Without another word I hurried out past the dog drooling in the corner. I went out the front, a luxury most burglars never get. Strapped the box into the back of the El Camino with some twine. A minute later I was a mile down the road.

Took Lovecraft's box back to my room at the Pink Flamingo, sat it on the floor and stared at it for five seconds before collapsing onto the horsehair blankets and falling asleep. I had a lot of strange dreams that night I chalked up to nerves. I dreamt I was being forced to eat that steak with the Nembutals buried inside. I could taste the bitter pills and the raw meat and it was enough to make me gag. I dreamt that I was trapped in some sort of jail. Dark, all I could feel were the bars, the cold metal. Finally I dreamt of my mother and that was the most disturbing dream of all. Because I dreamt that I scalped her and scooped out her brains with a wide spoon and ate them until they were gone. I felt the shame of what I'd done. Like it was real.

Woke about eight am covered in sweat from my night terrors and looked at the ironwood box and it just sat there and yet somehow it felt... I guess the word for it would be sentient... but I'm not the kind of fairy would use a word like that in conversation. It felt like the trunk was staring back at me. I had no real interest in peering inside, I told myself. I was a deliveryman, nothing more.

I was eating my breakfast, eggs poached in boiling water on a hot plate and a can of those Vienna sausages along with about a pot of coffee. Anyways I was about halfway through breakfast when the telephone rang. You ever notice when you are about to get bad news on the telephone you have some sort of gut feeling about it? Like someone reached inside your belly and got your intestines all knotted up? I knew right away it wasn't a call I wanted to answer.

Hello? I says.

A man with a thick German accent answers. Gute morgen, he says.

Good morning, I says to him.

I know vat you hev, the man says. I spoke to Professor Antone.

Who is this? I ask.

I'm a writer. A writer who does his research. And I would very much like to pay you for Calliope. More money than that girl from Maine's got.

Who the hell is Calliope? I says.

Mein Got. Have you not opened it? Did you not ask Antone what was inside?

I was paid to fetch it, I says. Not open it. So listen to me. I'm not selling what's inside. What I'm selling is the opportunity to open it yourself. You want in? Fine. Get in line. Money talks and all that.

Ten, cash, he says. But it has to be tonight.

Ten thousand dollars was more than I earned my last year on the force. Twice and then some. A lot of coin for a man like me. Enough maybe to retire on if I played it right. Enough maybe for a down payment on that cabin I was eyeing on the Cape. I didn't have to think too long.

Where? I ask.

I come to you, he says. We should say... six o'clock?

Do you have it? the kid asks soon as the operator connects us. I was on the pay phone outside the Pink Flamingo, one of those old glass cages nobody uses anymore. Like where Superman changes. Where do you suppose he changes, now? Dunno. Where was I? Right. The kid. I call her collect all the way to Maine. I was that kind of guy then.

Well kid it's like this, I says. I've got good news and I've got bad news. What do you want first?

Um... I guess the good... she says.

Good news is I have your treasure chest. It's real and there's something inside but I don't know what and it's in my room right now.

That's boss! says the kid. What about the bad news?

The bad news is the price just went up. You ain't the only person interested in this thing anymore.

There was a long silence on the other end of the line. When she spoke again her voice got all funny. The kid was pouting. We had a deal, she says. You signed a contract.

I signed a piece of paper sure, I says.

That's not fair.

Then let me be the first person to tell you something...

We don't have any more money, she says. You know all that we had was that three grand. It took us forever to save.

Play me a fuckin fiddle, I says. As a courtesy I thought I'd offer you the chance to match the price before I hawked it. Part of me felt bad, sure. No honor among thieves as they say.

You can't do this, the kid says.

You gonna call the cops? I says. I was a cop. What would you tell them wouldn't implicate you in some way? In case you didn't know what you paid me to do wasn't exactly legal. So we'll just call it even stevens. I'll keep the fifteen hundred already paid for expenses and whatnot. You can keep the other half and buy your mom a car.

Money's got nothing to do with what I want here, the kid says. She was stammering, trying to figure out, I guess, how to keep me on the horn.

Nothing has nothing to do with money, I says.

Look, the box... this thing is more complicated. Calliope.

Yeah I head that name earlier today, I says. Calliope. It's a manu-script, right? The title of a lost Lovecraft novel, something you can put your name on and make riches?

And then the kid says something real funny. She says, It's going to be rooting around in your head looking for your memories.

This non sequitur made no sense to me at the time. But it made me think about the dreams I'd had the night before. I thought about that dream about my mother, in particular. But that wasn't a memory. That was a nightmare.

Don't get cranked, I says. Maybe nothing's in the box, anyway. Maybe just an old sweater, some old notes.

It's in there, she says. Why else would they be after it? Why else would this guy pay you so much?

I don't know kid. People are funny.

It's meant for me, she says. If you don't bring it up here I'm afraid some people might get hurt.

Are you threatening me? I ask the kid.

No, man. I'm warning you. She's gotta be real hungry. If she doesn't have the right memories to eat she's going to look for something else.

Do us both a favor, I told her. Go see a head shrinker. You're not making any sense.

The German wore a gray wool suit and smelled like Germolene. Said his name was Calvin and his family hailed from somewhere south of Dresden. I didn't tell him that twenty years before you and I had visited Dresden and killed ten krauts looked just like him. I think he knew. I brought him into my room at the Pink Flamingo and he took a seat on the bed and I took the chair. He carried a thick attaché case nearly bursting at the seams. It was cram-packed with twenty-dollar bills. The man didn't waste no time.

That it? he asks. He points to the thing under the blanket against the wall. Something the size and shape of a baby's coffin.

That's it, I says.

I was getting concerned about this man because he had arrived alone. He had arrived alone carrying ten G's cold cash. That made one of us stupid. Either he was stupid for not bringing backup or I was stupid for letting this guy into my room because maybe his agenda was something a little more steely. Maybe this was a man who could do some murdering outside the theater of war and not blink. Did we blink when we killed those krauts? Maybe he thought he could take the money, take the box, and make off with everything?

My nine was in its holster under my left arm. But he was big, and fast, this man, pure-blood Eastern European stock, good ol' Aryan boy. Kind they don't make no more. And like I said, I'd grown old and fat. I was more than a little worried to tell the truth.

Why do you want this thing so bad? I ask, trying to draw him into some sort of conversation till I could suss out his motives.

I've been a Lovecraft scholar for some time, he says. All the way back to University. I've analyzed his writings, all of his notes and I can tell you there was no better writer during his time. In fact, no better writer since Edgar Allan Poe. Their writing contained something... unique. An outside perspective of the human condition not present in the works of their contemporaries.

You'll have to excuse me, I says. But I'm just a dumb dude from Veazie. I didn't take no English classes at the polytechnic, if you catch my drift. I was too busy saving the world. So I'm not exactly sure what the hell half of what you just said really means.

The man laughs. Let me put it like this, he says. There is something *magical* about their stories. Something too perfect. I came to believe that they were helped a bit. Assisted. Lovecraft and Poe.

Then the German tells me how, six years ago, he was looking through Poe's archives in Baltimore when he discovered a series of letters Poe had written to his cousin. In case you didn't know, Poe married his first cousin, sick fuck. He wrote a series of letters to her when they were courting. One of the letters described a hasty journey the author took to Rome in 1854. Poe made curious mentions of a woman, Calliope, the German says. But my research leads me to believe that this Calliope he referred to was no woman at all.

I just wanted him to give me the money and skedaddle. That's what I was thinking. Suddenly I wanted the box out of my hotel room. I never wanted to see it again.

Then the Germ asks me, Does she talk to you?

Who? I says.

Calliope. Does she sing at you?

I don't know what you are talking about, man, I tell him. Nobody's been talking to me.

Very good, he says. Then with kind of a nervous quiver he hands me the attaché case. I take it like it's no big deal and pull the zipper back a bit. Tommy Jefferson winked at me and I closed her up tight. I could count it later.

Let us then have a look, he says, and he makes for the chest.

No refunds, I says. You open that thing in here and all you find inside is a Cracker Jack prize this money is still mine. Caveat emptor. That's the only Latin I know.

Yes, he laughs. Well played, well played. The money is yours.

And with that the German walks over to the box and pulls the linen off.

Do you have the key? he asks.

Do I have the... no! Do I have the fucking key? I didn't buy it at Woolworths, man.

Americans, he says. Always so angry. He reaches into his suit jacket and I kind of tense up for a second and put a hand on my nine, expecting him to bring out anything from a piano wire to a Colt 45 but all that's in his hand is a bit of copper wire which he gently sets into the locking mechanism in the front of the ironwood chest. I watch him dig around in there and I think, for just a second I think I hear something. Like a low shifting of weight somewhere and maybe even a short vocalization. Something like *Pim*. Just a single word – *Pim*. If there really was a sound, the German didn't catch it because he didn't hesitate. He just kept digging into the lock. And after only twenty seconds I heard a click like an invitation.

Ah, he sighs. He puts his back to me and blocks my view of the box. He wants this first glimpse to be his. It seems to me that he felt this moment was romantic. Romantic like the way a serial killer might find an abduction romantic if you catch my drift. Anyway I sit in the chair and watch his back and see his hands move and then he slowly opens it up. The lid creaks on hinges that hadn't opened in who knows how long. The last man to open it had probably been ol' H.P. himself.

Something happened. Like something I skipped over. My head's fuzzy about it even now. But the next thing I remember after the German opened that box, is a loud pounding. It was like – you ever been to one of those films at the Majestic that had already been out for six months? One of the films they had to patch? You're sittin there watching the *French Connection* or something and then you get to a spot that must have broken down before when one of the projectionists slacked on the job or went outside for his cigarette break... like sometime in the past the film got all fucked up and they had to chop out two seconds of the movie so what you get is kind of a jump cut is what they call it. Your characters are in one scene halfway through a conversation and then you get to that part in the film that was broken and now it's gone and now your characters are in some other place? And there's this loud sound when the twisted film passes over the sound head. That's what it was like.

One second I was standing there watching the German open the box and the next... the next, all I hear was this constant pounding, this loud pounding of a fist upon the door to my hotel room. And then someone

33

screaming on the other side of the door, yelling at me, shouting, Are you ok in there? Is everything ok? Please open the door!

I looked around as I came back to myself. The room, man. The room was painted with the German's blood. I mean, painted. And it wasn't just blood. Goddamn intestines dangled from the overhead fan. The German's decapitated head was propped up on the dresser top like a cookie jar from Hell. His blank eyes stared back at me. A foot, his severed fucking foot rested in my lap. Everywhere was blood. So much blood. It was on my clothes. I could feel it in my hair. It had soaked into the carpet. It made sucking sounds when I walked across the room. I had never seen so much blood. Not in the war. Not on the force. I looked around. A moan escaped me and I thought I might begin to scream too so I bit down on my cheek. I looked back to the box. The lid was closed.

Hello? The voice from the other side of the door. Are you okay? Is everybody okay in there? And more of that pounding.

I ignored it and stepped toward the German's severed head because I noticed something strange about it, other than the fact it has been detached from its body. A large hole had been drilled into the German's skull above where his eyebrows creased, right there in the middle. A hole about the size of a silver dollar, the Eisenhower. God help me, I looked in the hole. His skull was scraped clean like a hollowed-out pumpkin.

It was a frame-up. That's what I decided right away; somebody was framing me for the German's murder. I'd walked myself into a situation I didn't understand, some international scheme. I'd been drugged, obviously. Gas. Must have been gassed and then someone had come in and murdered the German and framed me for the job. But why? And who?

Knock. Knock. Knock. Is everything all right in there? the man says again.

Go away! I shout.

I heard a lot of noise in there! he says. It sounded like fighting, is everybody all right?

I said go away!

I gotta call the cops, the man says. If you don't come out I gotta call the cops.

I couldn't open the door into to this massacre so I says, Do what you got to do.

I stumble into the bathroom, then, searching for some kind of back exit, a window, anything. There's a window but it's barely wide enough to reach my arm through.

I double back, slipping on a piece of the German's large intestine that had fallen to the floor. It made a sound under my shoe almost like a child's squeak toy as trapped gas escaped. I nearly lose my balance but manage to catch myself by grabbing the edge of the wall. There, my fingerprints in blood. Perfect. I hurry around, grabbing my things, packing what I can. I'm out of time. The police will be here any second. I strip off my gore-soaked clothes and do a piss-poor job washing my hands and face before putting on a fresh pair of Levi's and a raggedy t-shirt I'd brought along.

I pry the German's attaché case from under a mass of angel-wing organs might have been lungs. I yell a little when I look inside the case. Resting on a stack of twenty-dollar bills is an ear. Blood has soaked through most of that bundle. I carefully toss the ear, making sure not to get my hands bloodied again. I unwrap the ruined bills and drop them on the floor. Now it looks like a burglary gone horribly wrong. Perhaps that was part of their plan too, whoever gassed me and set me up.

I'm almost to the door when I remember Lovecraft's box. I look back. I don't know if I can carry both the case and the box at the same time. I go to the ironwood chest and lift it and I don't know if it was the adrenaline or the nerves kicking in or what but the box is suddenly lighter. I pick it up with the attaché case wrapped around one shoulder and I make for the door.

I throw the door open wide and jog to my El Camino. The inquisitive fella who done the pounding is standing in the entryway of the motel office about fifty feet from my room.

Hey! Hey you! he shouts.

I ignore him and open the cab of the car and push the attaché case over onto the passenger seat. Then I put the ironwood chest in the bed and strap it tight with the twine I keep under a spare tire.

Hey mister, what the hell happened in there? he shouts at me. And now the ruddy Irish motel clerk is with him and they're both walking to me. They pass the open door to my room and their heads swivel and take in the scene and then both of them together back away towards the office again, hands raised.

We don't want no trouble, amigo, the clerk says like I look Mexican or somethin.

I didn't say nothin. Knew there was nothing to say. Nothing to say to them, nothing to say to the police that would convince them I hadn't been the one to lobotomize that German. The backwater corn-pone cops wouldn't never believe somebody set me up. Because what was the motive? Even I didn't know. Wasn't the money – I had the cash. Wasn't the box – I had that, too. Maybe they just wanted the German dead. Maybe he'd crossed someone. Whatever it was I didn't have time to go lookin for an answer.

I tried to figure out my next move but for the first fifteen minutes of my escape I couldn't think of nothin. My mind kept going blank like there was something wrong with my starter, like my solenoids weren't firing.

I figure by the time I stopped for gas, the police had found the room, gone over it, found my fingerprints in the German's blood. Nowadays that would have been all she wrote. But back then things were different. Lot less organized. The police out there couldn't feed my prints into a central computerized system. Wouldn't have somethin like that for decades. My prints believe it or not weren't even filed with Portland P.D. where I used to work. Nobody ever thought to print the police. To pin the prints on me they'd have to catch me first and compare a fresh set to what they'd lifted from the scene of the crime. I had paid cash at the Pink Flamingo and didn't nobody care who stayed in motels back then so they didn't have my name. Might be they got my plates though and if they did I would be in a bind when the detectives traced the car back to my place in Veazie. My experience with eyewitnesses of violent crimes though told me the odds were heavily in my favor. When confronted with terror nobody remembers to remember details like license plates. Still, if someone dug hard enough, they'd find me, sure. I'd left a lot of loose ends back there, not the least of which was the drooling woman from the diner. All the case needed was one smart detective. I was just beginning to sweat it when I remembered Bijou.

Bijou means *kiss* in French and this man was a Frenchman and that's what he called himself. Once upon a time he lived in Portland two doors down from me where he'd run a brothel that had employed fine, clean women. He ran into some trouble with the Cumberland County Sheriff, though. So Bijou, he came to me and I helped him get set up south of Boston in a town called Whitman.

Bijou was running his business out of an abandoned family campground, the kind with those squat, square cottages that really are only but one room not even a shitter. It was called the Gentlemen's Pleasure and he advertised it as a health spa for distinguished men. Of course everybody knew the game. Only difference between what he was doing down Whitman and what he done up in Portland was in Whitman the cops knew how to go along to get along.

I needed to ditch my El Camino much as I loved her. That chariot got me out of a few tight binds but she was too showy. And I couldn't take the chance one of them guys back at the Pink Flamingo really did get my plates. I needed something low key. Bijou could help with that. He owed me.

I'm pretty sure on the way to Whitman that I heard something inside the box making sounds. And it sounded like some sound only I could hear. You know what I mean? Like it wasn't coming from without but within.

Pim, it says. Or I thought it said. *Pim*, it sang. And then a new sound, something like, *Tekeli-li! Tekeli-li!* It sounded almost like a bird's song.

◆ ◆ ◆

Bijou was a big fat Frenchman, guy like me. Except he had kinky black hair and a soul patch instead of a goat-tee.

He called himself a Quebecois. Maybe he was. Maybe he wasn't. All I know is that he was in Montreal for a minute before moving south through the States. In Whitman, he lived in this kind of a large plantation house on top a hill that overlooked the Gentleman's Delight cottages. When I pulled in he was standing right out front to greet me.

Ah, Michelle, he says as I climb out of the El Camino.

It's Michael, Bijou, I tell him for the hundredth time.

Ah Michelle, Michelle, come in, we'll have a sweet tea.

I don't have time for that right now, I says.

Oh, well then make time.

So I follow him into the house. His home was stupid with that cherry wainscoting and stank of Murphy's Oil Soap. Reminded me of the Catholic School where I went to Kindergarten. Inside, I see one of his girls on her hands and knees scrubbing at the banister going upstairs. She looks at me and smiles and nods her head as I pass by and when she does I see she has a tooth missing up front.

Bijou takes me to a dining room where there's a roll top desk set up behind a long table. Seemed like this was where he conducted the majority of his business, at least the stuff he dared to record on paper. He sits behind the desk and I take one of the chairs. He whistles at the girl at the banister and she hurries away into the kitchen. A moment later I hear the sounds of clinking glass and ice being chopped up with a pick.

Michelle, what on earth has happened? he asks.

I thought about that for a moment not really sure how to answer and finally settled on the truth or at least as much I knew of it at the time. He was earthbound. I could trust him.

It's a frame-up, I says. Don't know why. Don't know who. But some cops are going to think I murdered somebody.

He shakes his head. Too bad you did not dispatch this man here in Whitman, he says. If you'd taken him here, I have friends could make that go away, but up Providence? No I don't think so. Not unless you're Italian.

I gotta ditch the car, I says. I'll need a new ride. And some place to hole up for the night. I should go to ground.

Bijou nods. You know up in Portland, he says, we didn't have the cops but we didn't have the family. Down here we've got the cops but we also have the family.

I don't understand.

We are close enough to Providence it's become a bit of a problem. Every year their tithe goes up, you know?

La Cosa Nostra? I says.

Yes, *this little thing of theirs*, they call it. They come down here and make a scene maybe scare the girls if I don't send them twenty points first Tuesday each month.

You behind? I ask.

I'm always behind. This recession. You know how it is. Sex, drugs, booze. Sex is the first sin to go when times get tough. You got enough drugs or booze, you can still have sex with the old lady, sans blague.

I nod to pacify. I don't mean to sound insincere Bijou but I'm pressed for time, I says.

Ah yes, yes, quite right. Your car. He whistles again and the woman at the banister comes in with a tray of drinks. She serves one to Bijou and hands me the other. It's a tall glass of homemade ice tea sweating with condensation. This is Cinnamon, says Bijou.

She smiles at me. Then she says something light in a clipped but fluid language and I knew that she couldn't really understand what we were saying.

She is Russian, says Bijou. Come over on the boat, friend of the family's. The real family, my family – back home.

So what's her real name then? I ask.

Her real name is Cinnamon, he said with a shrug. I don't know what it means in Russian. I don't know if it's Cinnamon like cinnamon, like the cinnamon that we have – the kind we put in gravy, I don't know. She says she's Cinnamon, I call her Cinnamon.

Hello Cinnamon, I said.

Cinnamon here will help you get to Quincy. Got a guy there owns a body shop; he'll take care of you. El Camino will be no more; it's a sad thing, yes?

It is, I like that car.

Go with Cinnamon, he tells me. She knows where you're going. Then he says something in Russian and Cinnamon walks out the front door without another word. I stand up, shake Bijou's hand.

One more thing, I says.

Yes, anything old friend.

That box in the back of the El Camino, I says. I need to leave it here till we come back.

Yes, it will be safe here. What's inside?

Don't know.

Okay, yes, he says. Anything else?

Yes. Please don't open it.

Bijou looked offended. Sorry, I says. It's just been awhile since I've been around a friend.

When I stepped outside, Cinnamon was waiting in the El Camino legs barely long enough to reach the floor. She looked like a kid. Probably was. I walked over to the car and offloaded the chest and brought it back into the house. Put it in a storage closet under the stairs, right in the hallway. I gave it one final glance and I don't know what it was but I just had a bad feeling. I shook it off though. There were all sorts of reasons I should have had a bad feeling that day not the least of which was that damned ironwood chest.

Back in the car I moved the moneybag under my legs and looked to Cinnamon. She pointed down the drive. She didn't talk much on the way there. She looked out the window and whistled through the gap of her missing tooth.

◆ ◆ ◆

I'm not taking no goddamn Nazi car, I tell the fella at the body shop when I seen what he has waiting for me.

It's all I got, Daddy-O, he says. Or you can get back in your El Camino and scram. I owe Bijou, yessir, but not enough to take your shit. You can D.D.T. far as I'm concerned.

The car was a clunky Volkswagen the kind looked like a bubble of a spaceship cruising down the highway. It was green, that dark green knotty pines get before it rains. Cab was rusted around the wheel wells but the wheels themselves looked solid.

It's not a fair trade, I says.

I say it was? he says. Guy was a skinny man lousy with grease on his duck butt wearing those khaki overalls. And he had a half beard like Amish men sometimes wear but I didn't get the drift he was Amish.

I kicked one of the back tires playfully because I didn't know what else to do and finally resigned myself. Shook the mechanic's hand and then walked to my El Camino to give her one last look over. I picked the change outta the cup holder and fished my sig from the glove compartment along with a box of nines and then I took the German's attaché case back to the crummy Volkswagen. I climbed in the passenger seat and kind of sat on the case itself while Cinnamon got behind the wheel. Figured she'd like to drive it back. I was too sour to try her out myself just yet.

On the way back Cinnamon talked a lot but I understood hardly none of it. She was a real jabberjaw once she got used to you. She rambled on and on and on but all I could make out was a single word, *Shoshanna*. I assumed it was a sister or her mother because every time she'd mention this Shoshanna she'd get tears in the corners of her eyes. I knew how to listen to women and in the pauses when she glanced sideways at me at the end of a sentence I nodded and smiled or maybe grunted a little. I liked the sound of her voice.

By the time we got back to Whitman she was laughing and chatting away like we were the best of friends. We pulled into Gentlemen's Delight right before sunset. I don't know what it was about the lay of the place. I knew right away something was wrong. All of Bijou's women had gathered at the big house, on the porch steps. They chattered in three different languages. As I got close they backed up a ways and I saw what lay in the middle. It was Bijou. He was bent backwards over the top step. An older bronze-skinned woman nursed his wounds. She held a washcloth wrapped round a bundle of ice to his bottom lip. His right eyelid was cut open and it bled a steady stream. He grimaced when he saw me and I knew right away Lovecraft's box was gone.

I'm so sorry my friend, he says. So sorry, so very sorry.

Bijou, what the hell? I ask.

It was those goombas, come down outta Providence, pay a visit, ask for money. I have no money. I have no money to give them. I tell them this over the phone and they come down anyways.

And they took the box? I ask. 'Course I already knew the answer.

They took the box, he says. They took lots of things. I'm sorry; they thought it was valuable. I couldn't talk them out of it even when I tell them it wasn't mine. They tried to open it but nothing would open it. They said they had special tools back at the office and then they took it with them when they left.

I just stand there a beat, taking in the whole story. I nod. Then I walk over to Bijou and I grab him. Grab him by the cuff of his shirt. Grab him so tight I probably yanked out some chest hairs. I lift him up like a sack of flour then I ram him into the side of his whorehouse. I grab the hair just above his forehead and slam his skull back against the siding slats.

Bijou, you motherfucker, I says. Did you forget who I am?

I told them not to take it, he says.

Bullshit. You called them the second I was gone and you told them to come down here and settle your debts.

No... no. I would never...

I pull out my nine and the girls scream and scatter. I put it up to Bijou's temple and pull back the hammer with my thumb. Generally, I'm a gracious man, but I have no sympathy for turncoats. They kind of make me insane.

You stupid frog, I says. I'm going to count to ten and somewhere in there I'm going to blow your fucking head off. One...

Michelle... I swear...

Two. And call me Michelle again you stupid fuck.

I didn't mean to... I didn't think... I didn't think it through...

Three. What are you trying to tell me Bijou? Four.

You're right! he screams. You're right. I called them. I called them. I'm so sorry, my friend. I'm so sorry. I owe them so much money you don't know. I can't run anymore. I'm too old.

I pulled the sidearm away from his head, settled the hammer, put it in the waistband of my jeans. Where? I ask. Where'd they take it? Providence?

Boston, he says.

Time to get specific.

They took it to Parma, he says.

Parma, Parma, what's that? Is that some sort of... what section of Boston is that? I never heard of Parma.

Parma, it's a place, Bijou says. It's a restaurant.

I start to walk away. Wait, he says. You cannot go there.

The hell I can't. That's my property. At least it is as long as it's between places.

But these men, he says. These men are not nice people Michelle, they're not like us. They will hurt you.

I've been hurting for years, I says.

Then shoot low, he says. Those guys're riding Shetlands.

On the way back to the car Cinnamon runs up to me and presses something into the palm of my hand.

As I pull out of the drive in that shitty green Volkswagen bug I open my hand to see what she'd given me. It was a simple Jesus cross made of

JAMES RENNER - MUSE

white gold. It had once been a necklace but the necklace part of it was gone. I wasn't exactly sure what it meant but I tucked it into my pocket and kept it with me.

◆ ◆ ◆

Dominick Gallucci Sr. ran the mafia in Providence about five years. Social climber with a car bomb fetish. Got the gig by blowing up four Capos. Car bombs got very easy to make right around that time using those radios you could pick up in any neighborhood electronics store. You get a transistor in the hands of a dago like Gallucci and sure as shit you got a blood feud on your hands.

Here's a story bout Gallucci don't know if it was true probably was. Word from the bird was that Gallucci took a hit out on ol Foster Furcolo couple years before this. Furcolo was threatening to take away some corporate garbage contract the Gallucci family were consulting on. Didn't happen a'course but Gallucci went so far as to bring a gunman up from Florida to do the hit. And even though the hit never happened Gallucci had the hitman rubbed out to cover his tracks. Body was found in Buzzards Bay. Guy like that. Guy who wouldn't think nothin of killin a governor just cause. Guy like that doesn't necessarily negotiate, you know?

In 1960 Gallucci kept an office in the kitchen of this Parma family joint that was down in Cambridge, sort of a criminal Italian embassy in the middle of mick country. Before I went over I ducked into a cheap motel on the other side of Harvard Yard. Paid the receptionist cash keeping my eyes on my shoes the whole time. In the room, I ditched the cheese, stuffed the German's attaché case under the bed.

I walk into Parma late that same evening. The dinner crowd is thinning out. Big fat Italian women and their big fat husbands and their big fat kids crowd round tables covered in white and red checkered cloth. In the corner some Methuselah plays at a fiddle. His Sophie plays the squeezebox. The receptionist she looks vaguely familiar to me although I'd never been to this part of town and I'd certainly never met Gallucci before though I'd heard of him.

You have message for me, she says, the receptionist. It was a thick Soviet accent.

You have message for me, she repeats. From Cinnamon.

Cinnamon's your sister?

She laughs at this. We are coo-zins. You have message for me?

I pull out the white gold cross and hand it over. A single tear tumbles out of her eye down her cheek and she mumbles something could have been *So, he was here after all,* before falling silent again.

I need to see…

I know who you are here to see but he does not wish to see you Mister Hadley. I am sorry, thank you for the message.

Is he in the kitchen? I ask pointing to the swinging doors in the back of the restaurant.

Her eyes go wide and she looks at me, waiting to see if I dare confront the man in his castle. I walk deliberately across the room. The evening diners are too focused on their plates of capellini and heavy gravy to pay attention to another fat guy strolling through the restaurant. I push through the swinging door and arrive in the kitchen, a noisy stainless steel place full of Italian men in aprons most of them with pencil-thin black mustaches and older than dirt.

See him immediately at the back of the kitchen by the walk-in freezer. Dominic Gallucci sitting at a wood table smaller than he is picking at a plate of linguini and clams. He was a hairy fellow with some muscles. He looks up at me and then he looks to a man standing next to him who at first I think is a particularly tall cook but it turned out it was Gallucci's personal bodyguard, fellow by the name of Anthony Callibrese. Callibrese steps my way and I can tell by how he walks that a confrontation is coming. Gallucci didn't want to talk.

Don't come any closer, I says. And for just a second Callibrese stops in his tracks. The kitchen goes quiet. All the pots and pans stop clanging, all the plates stop being plated. Nobody moves a fork. Only sound can be heard is the hum of the refrigerator unit and the sizzle of calamari in the deep fryer.

Mr. Gallucci has nothing for you, the giant says to me.

He's got my property, I says. I don't have anything to do with Bijou's debts.

Callibrese moves for me. I had my sidearm but I didn't want a gunfight. The only other weapon within reach was a long pair of metal tongs they were using to set some meat on a brasserie. I snatch the tongs out of the cook's hand and poke Callibrese in the chest with them.

Stand back, I says. Callibrese tries to grab the tongs away and I stab him again in the stomach this time harder. It knocks the wind out of his lungs.

All right, he says and this time he manages to snatch away the tongs. For a second there I begin to have some doubts. Callibrese comes at me again and this time he gets me. Grabs me by the front of the shirt and pushes me back as hard as he can. I go skidding across the floor. My head collides with the sink and all sorts of utensils rain down around me. A waiter cuts into the kitchen to see what the hub-bub is and then just stands there like a spaz.

I pick myself up as Callibrese turns away. I ain't done with you, I says. This time Callibrese is faster, he comes at me like a thrown dart. I swing round groping for anything within reach. This time it's a frying pan. It collides with the giants' head with a pleasant *thunk*. Does nothing more than stun him for two seconds. In that time I grab a pot of what I think is boiling water and throw it on his chest. But they had just added the water to the stovetop and it wasn't even warm. In fact, it was mighty cold and Callibrese shivered a little before he set his eyes back on me.

You finished? he says.

I guess that's it, I tell him.

Callibrese smiles. But when he steps forward his shoe slips in the puddle of water at his feet and it knocks him off balance. He tries to catch himself with his left hand. I think for a second that he'll be just fine but he'd built up some momentum and it shifted his weight in an unexpected way. His left hand slips off the grill and goes right into the bubbling fryer. His arm sinks elbow-deep and he begins to scream like a girl.

Callibrese pulls his arm out and looks at it. We both watch the white blisters pop up across his skin like fresh little pork rinds. I could hear the crackling. An older cook runs to him and tosses a bowl of flour across his arm and pulls Callibrese away.

I turn back to Gallucci but he's just sitting there chewing his pasta and then he does a kind of a shrug and reaches under the table and when he brings out his hand he's holding a gun very much like my own. I hear the shot before I can react, like he threw thunder at me and I feel the bullet punch through my body.

The dining room was empty by the time they drug me back there. I guess everyone left when they heard the gunshot. I was at a booth and Shoshanna, Cinnamon's cousin, was patching me up best she could with fishing line and some gauze and ace bandages and some peroxide they kept in stock. The bullet had gone in and out through the muscle above my left armpit.

The wife says I can't kill you, Dominic says to me. Dominic is sort of pacing around a tiled square and as he circles, he wraps his hand in bright white tape. When he's done he slips on a boxers' glove. Not the red kind you see in movies but the smaller sort. And brown not red.

I can't kill you, he says. So I'm going to fuck you up a little bit.

I nod and Shoshanna ducks out. Callibrese stands there watching kind of pouting over his burned arm. Dominic steps to me, his expensive leather shoes tap, tapping on the tile floor. Then his arm shoots out from his body and his fist connects with my left cheekbone. I feel something snap and there's a bright explosion of pain. Firecrackers in my head.

Dominic pants, looks at me, considers my face a moment and then brings his fist down again. KAPOW! I feel blood drip off my face. I feel the drop-lets hitting my thighs, saturating my pants.

Dominic brings his hand back again, building up juice for another hit.

Wait, I says.

What?

Could you switch sides? Just looks funny to have one side all smashed and the other all smooth.

Dominic thinks about this a second. Yeah sure you bet, he says. He walks around my other side and then brings his right fist down, not so much in an arc but more top to bottom, connecting with my right cheek. I feel it pop out of place. I black out for a second, not long.

Finally Dominic rests and stands, wiping the sweat off his caveman forehead. He takes off the boxing glove and sits across from me.

Where's the box? I ask.

He laughs. It's not yours anymore, he says. It never really was yours anyways I guess.

I can't leave here without it, I says.

No sooner had those words escaped my lips, the screaming begins. It starts with the screams of a young woman. Not Shoshanna, somehow I knew that. Some other woman, a high caterwauling scream. The kind can only mean murder. Then it's joined by a chorus of shrieks. These were mostly men but still high-pitched, final primal screams. We hear a great thudding above us as people scramble around on the second floor. There's scraping, chairs being pushed, thrown against the wall, glass breaking, bodies falling to the ground, more screams and finally worst of all – silence.

Dominic looks to me. I look at the bodyguard. Nobody moves a muscle for what seems an eternity. Then Shoshanna comes running from the kitchen. She doesn't even look at us. She runs right out the door. As far as I know she never stopped. Maybe she ran all the way back to Ukraine.

We run upstairs, the three of us. I follow Dominic and the bodyguard through the kitchen, first. Behind the sink was a flight of narrow wooden steps leading to an apartment. Up top is a door and Dominic throws it open and we stumble inside.

It was a massacre. Must have been six or seven people to begin with. Impossible to count; their limbs...most of their limbs were no longer attached to bodies. And it was hard to distinguish how they matched up with the arms and legs in the haphazard pile in the center of the room. Things dripped. You couldn't not hear it. Organs smacked to the floor like big gooey drops of rain. And there against the far wall among a patch of floor that was still clean was Lovecraft's box.

I think I was the only one who saw what I saw – the only one who saw the thing inside the ironwood chest because the lid hadn't quite shut when we come into the room. There was a space of about six inches as the lid was closing and in that space I saw an arm. A short stubbly gray arm and at the end of it a hand with fingers like talons. I watched it slip inside the box and then the lid shut tight.

Memory is funny thing isn't it Bill? We can deny so much that we know to be true. I think that's what I started to do after seeing that gray hand with the taloned fingers.

What happened? says Dominic. What happened? He keeps saying that over and over like a broken record. It's all that he could say.

It was a... it was a bomb, says the bodyguard.

But there was no explosion, he says.

Look at their bodies, Callibrese says and then he stumbles back against the wall and his eyes rolled up into his head and he slips to the ground, the oxygen having run out of his small brain.

What happened? Dominic says again. He kneels in a pool of blood and reaches out and touches the remains of some loved one, this piece an indistinguishable bit of flesh. The head lays nearby, its skull cracked open, the inside hollow or mostly.

What happened? says Dominic.

I cross the room, my shoes leaving a trail in the congealing blood. I pick up the ironwood chest and walk past Dominic and down the stairs. I don't think he even knew I was gone. We were both in shock, anyway.

What happened? His voice trailed after me.

Found my Volkswagen behind the restaurant. The cops would be coming soon no doubt. I needed to get gone. I know what you're wondering – why am I not frightened of that ironwood chest – but I wasn't thinking about the thing inside at that moment. My good sense denied it. My mind pushed it away. I wasn't thinking about anything other than the fact that the box represented another fifteen hundred dollars to me if I could still deliver it to the kid. Fifteen C notes on top of what was left in the German's attaché case would set me up somewhere safe. The heat was coming. Witnesses could place me at the site of two violent murders. My arrest seemed inevitable. My mind was so unwilling to surrender to the fantastic that I carried a box filled with some unimaginable evil as if it held nothing more than old clothes.

There was just enough room to tuck the box behind the bucket seats of the old Bug. Soon I was driving out of Cambridge through the twisted be-damned streets of Boston searching for a highway, any highway. I escaped onto Route 90 West. I was driving blindly with no destination. I only knew I couldn't stay in Boston. It wasn't safe yet to head north to the kid, not if the police were looking for me. Better to lay low for a few days. Go to ground. Get my face to healing. Everybody notices a man with a busted mug.

I was so exhausted by then, by the events of the day and the pain that now agitated my entire body like a surging current from a wayward telephone line. I'd been shot. Beaten good. I'd been witness to great depravity, the likes of which I thought we'd left behind in Dachau. I drove west, blindly west, for how far I didn't know.

Sometime much later I came to the town of Holyoke and I got off the highway. My eyes were swelling shut and it was getting hard to see. I turned down a wide country lane following an arrow on a crude shingle

JAMES RENNER - MUSE

that had been placed at a crossroads and which advertised *Room to Let*. At the end of the lane was a farmhouse overlooking a pasture of cows and beyond the cows was an orchard of apple trees. I stopped there and limped to the front door hoping my bloodied, bruised face wasn't nearly as bad as it looked in the rearview.

A skinny country fellow answered the door. He wore bibbed overalls with nothing underneath. There was no hair on his chest and I judged him to be about thirty-five. He had one of those mustaches that was trying hard to be a mustache but not quite pulling it off – a ruddy kids' mustache. He looked at me and the bruises and the blood now soaking through the bandages around my left armpit, nodded and said, You're in some kind of trouble.

I nod back at him. Can I rent your room? I ask. Would that be a problem?

Does the trouble follow you? he asks me.

No sir, I lied.

Can you pay in cash?

I lay low at the Gorman farm for ten days and healed up some. They called it the Gorman farm though nobody there was named Gorman. Not anymore. Not for a long time. It was just the man, his old lady, and their kid. Girl about twelve years old. Tomboy of a girl with kind of scraggly blonde hair that hung to her shoulders and was never combed. She always wore jeans like a boy, a button-up shirt two sizes too big and suspenders to keep the shoulders down.

I carted Lovecraft's box up to the bedroom they were letting out on the second floor. All it was, was a bed with a couple blankets that were both thin and scratchy. In a corner was a chair-and-table set from some elementary school, one of those made-of-oak things where the top lifts up so you can store your paper and pencils inside. There was a window looked out to the cows, and beyond, the orchard.

51

Sat down for breakfast that first day and learned a little about each of them. Man's name was Landry. I assumed that was a last name though I never heard a first. The woman's name was Lynne and the girl they called Bobbi Jo. Their main source of income was the jugs of apple cider, hard and not, which they sold at a table set up a quarter a mile out by the main road. That pasture of cows I come to learn was no longer part of the farm and had been bought up by a neighbor five years before. The house belonged to Landry's family distantly and he had sort of inherited it after the death of a great uncle.

There was a shed round back where they made the cider, kind of a derelict shack that had once been painted the color of those Macintoshes but had weathered down to a spoiled brown. There was some sort of makeshift distillery in there made from a copper drum once used for moonshining. And the masher. This giant steam-powered contraption. Sort of machine that looked to me like it was always hungry for human fingers. The apples got mashed, some of the juice went to make the soft cider and the rest was distilled and fermented in the mash tun with the pulp.

The woman was always doing laundry and cooking and such. I often saw her hanging clothes out to dry through the window upstairs. She was pretty to look at; had a simple round face not too big. And she was kind although she didn't say much. She always gave me an extra helping of mashed taters at dinner.

Bobbi Jo was the one who picked the apples. She also mashed the apples, made the wort for the cider, cooked the cider. On Sundays she was the one that sold it down on the road. The only one I never actually saw working was Landry himself who usually roused at ten before shuffling onto the porch and clicking on the radio, listening to the Sox on WBUR. Sometimes he would recline under the willow tree out front and listen to AM radio broadcasts of evangelicals, the fire and brimstone kind you get out in them hills to this day. Every morning on his way out to the porch Landry would grab a jug of hard apple cider and by dinner the jug was empty.

It was hard for me to sleep at night. Looking back on it I think I probably had a concussion from the beating I took from Dominic. Though a part of it, an important part I guess, was the growing unease I felt for the ironwood chest. Lovecraft's box sat behind the door inside my room. It was locked and secure. I convinced myself I hadn't really seen what I thought I had seen up in that apartment above Parma. Only monsters I ever met were men. And lord there's enough of us not to need nothin more than that. But at night when it got dark and the only light was the moonbeams falling through that window, it shined on the ironwood and seemed to make it glow from the inside. And I wondered.

Sometimes I thought I heard something shift inside the ironwood chest. Like a baby adjusting itself in a womb.

I'm usually a man has everything nicely neat and ordered and it was also the disarray and unknowns that were keeping me awake. I didn't know how long I should stay at Gorman Farm before taking the box to the girl in Mechanic Falls. I dreamed that after it was done, I'd buy a tiki bar on the beach in that place down Mexico that I often dreamed of going.

And so for a spell I just waited for something to happen to make up my mind to get gone.

I need you to pick apples, Landry says to me the morning of my third day at Gorman Farm.

I shrugged and I says, Will it pay the tab?

I'll knock five dollars off, he says. For the week, not the day.

I nodded. Didn't have nothin else to do anyways I might as well make use of the hands God give me. So that morning I follow Bobbi Jo out to the orchard. The cows keep pace with us on their side of the fence as we walk. The girl doesn't talk but just sets up her ladder and goes to placing the mealy apples first into her apron and then bringing them down and unlatching bottom of the apron over one of the eight

53

tin buckets we brought along. They were those dented buckets probably made by hand, probably made by Landry's wife. Certainly not Landry himself.

I set up my ladder and get to picking. It's a lot harder than it looks. There's a certain way you have to twist an apple so the whole damn branch doesn't come off with it.

We're on our way back to the orchard the morning of my fourth day at Gorman Farm when Bobbi Jo finally says something.

You ever seen a penguin? she asks.

A penguin? Yeah sure I seen a penguin, I says. I've seen plenty of penguins.

She's quiet for a while and her question really starts to bother me.

Why do you want to know if I ever seen a penguin? I ask.

She shrugs. I guess I did see a penguin myself once, she says. It was at a menagerie when we lived in Mississippi. Meridian. My mama took me. My Da' came along. I seen a penguin but I don't remember it. Except last night I dreamt about it and it was just like she said this squat little bird and it looked like he had on a tuxedo like he was at some fancy dinner. You think that was a memory I don't remember having or do you think it was just a dream after all?

I don't say anything. Didn't seem like there was anything required to say. What did she want me to say about penguins?

You in school? I ask her later.

My mama schools me, she says.

And your Dad? What does he do?

Landry ain't my Da', she says. He's my stepda'. Daddy's down Folsom prison, will be there for another twenty I guess. Landry was his best friend.

What does Landry do? I ask.

Landry? You seen him. That's about what he does.

We stop in the shade of a willow tree just watchin the house. It was quiet I remember. A country quiet you never get in the city far way away from the hubbub and the ocean and all. A safe quiet.

What's it like? she asks.

What's it like?

Where you come from? What's it like?

Same as here. Not as pretty.

People do the same things up there?

People do the same things everywhere. All around the world. They just have different names for it. And don't never forget it. We're all the same. Just survivin. You'll see. So don't hurry it.

That night after dinner for the first time I hear Landry let into his old lady. I don't know if he had a belt or a bullwhip from the barn or what but he wasn't hitting her with his hands. It was making an awful noise and if I heard it I'm damn sure Bobbi Jo heard it too. Wish I could tell you I ran downstairs and treated him like a man. But I closed my eyes and covered my ears with my pillow and eventually I fell asleep.

I woke up later that night in the early morning it was dark outside still and for a moment I was sure someone was standing by the bed. Somebody only three feet tall, the size of a child. Startled, I sit up and look around at the room. It shines in the moonlight reflecting off the ironwood chest but nobody's there and the chest itself is still closed. I listen; the arguing and the beating has stopped. I can hear a clock ticking, the great-grandfather clock downstairs by the kitchen door. I can hear the machinery inside of it marking off the time. The gears of the clock like the gears of the world seemed to be stretched mighty thin and out of true.

I could hear sounds outside too. The long far off call of some animal, perhaps a coyote and the wind against the window where the eaves stuck out by my room. And then quite clearly I hear a word.

Pim?

The word is said like a question. My heart pounds in my chest. It's as though the word came from the ironwood chest. But I know how our minds play tricks on us especially the more isolated we are and the more quiet it is. Sometimes a man can imagine sounds that ain't there.

Pim? it says again. This time there's no fooling myself. It's an actual sound and it's coming from inside the box. I reach underneath the mattress and pull out my nine millimeter. I click back the hammer and get to my hands and knees and crawl over to Lovecraft's chest. I listen and I hear shifting inside, sandpaper drawn against the side of a grainy piece of wood and then that question again, *Pim?*

And then quite against my control and of no impulse of my own, I remember something. It's an old memory and at first it's a good memory. I was about five and I was in the living room of the house that we used to have over on Bellfonte Avenue. I was reading a comic book and my sister Janet who was only three at the time and could barely speak a dozen words was kneeling beside the coffee table coloring a picture of Howdy Doody. I remember that moment and then I remember what comes next and I cringe. I cringe in the present for what was coming out of the past.

In that memory, I finished my comic and set it down and looked around the room. My eyes happened upon a candy dish my mother kept on a bookshelf by the door. Inside the jar were peppermints and she kept them by the door so whenever she had company she could walk to it, open it up and give them a peppermint for the drive home. The dish itself had been a present from her mother's mother. Our great-grandmother who had died six months prior. At that moment I don't know why but I got a real hankering for one of those peppermints. Peppermints that Janet and I were never allowed to eat. I knew my mother was in the back bedroom hemming a skirt and I walked quietly over to the jar of candies and as I reached out and took it in my hands my mother must have moved in the bedroom because I heard a floorboard creak. Startled, I fumbled, and the dish from my great-grandmother fell to the floor where it broke into a hundred pieces.

The sound of the crash was enough to bring my mother running and it also brought Janet to her feet. My sister stood next to me over the shards of broken glass as my mother entered the room. My mother screamed. I remember my mother cried before she even asked any questions and when she did ask she looked at me and all I did was I pointed at Janet. Janet who was too young to understand what was taking place and certainly couldn't understand my betrayal. She picked Janet up, swatted her backside and took her to a bedroom where she stayed until late that evening when our father come home. I was never sure if that was when, if that was the turning point when our mother decided she didn't like Janet as much as me. But she always favored me. As an adult looking back on that moment so many years later I wondered how much of that was my fault. How much of that could be blamed on me. I got to thinking about all the little moments that make a life full of regret.

When I came back to the present I found myself kneeling in the bedroom next to ironwood chest. I had cried a little. And then I hear its voice again a kind of a gentle sound. A sound of a bird almost, the voice of a raven that can sing and talk at the same time.

Pim? it says to me. *Tekeli-li.* And this time I feel a trickle down the back of my neck as if a dead woman had touched me there and I spin around expecting some sort of monster with gray skin like the arm I had glimpsed slipping back into the box but nothing is there. But some invisible tentacle of electricity had found its way through my skin and it's tingling around the bottom of my head and I feel it slip inside and fill up my mind with fire.

Again I was taken back to that moment when I was a child and I relived the silly, sad memory as if I was there. The breaking of the candy dish and blaming my sister.

When I come back this time I hear a shifting, a definite shifting inside that ironwood chest. Something inside begins to purr. It purrs the way a large cat does after a big meal when they lay down in the sun for an afternoon nap.

Something come over me then and it's hard to explain what it was other than to say it was a *compulsion*. I run to the desk in a haze, the one borrowed from some elementary school and I sit down and open it up. Thank God there was paper and pencils stuffed inside because I don't know what I might have done otherwise. For the first time since I had been in school I begin to write a story. I write about that memory of breaking the dish except that's not exactly right because I change a couple things. I take it beyond what actually happened. And I realize in this one the boy grows up and tells his sister and apologizes for it and by doing so he understands something about himself. A little something about grace and forgiveness and in the end his sister forgives him even though their mother is long since dead. And somehow that makes them both – more. Makes them both more than they were before.

When I finally finish I see light playing on the horizon in the east through the window. I look down and I'm surprised to find six sheets of paper filled with my tiny handwriting. My hand aches where I had gripped the pencil tight. I read a bit of it. It was pretty much garbage. Not a lot of flowery words, none of that jackoff good writer stuff. I put the story back in the desk along with the pencils and the paper and I close it back up and slip back into bed.

It was going on noon when Bobby Jo shook me awake. I hadn't heard her come in. My fine-tuned instincts had weakened and that's a bad sign for a private eye. A sign it's time to maybe find a new career. Suppose it had been Gallucci's men. Or the law. They could have shot me in my sleep and I'd never known. Just woken up at the Pearly Gates, you know?

I let you sleep long as I could, says Bobby Jo. But we best get out to them apples. Tomorrow's Sunday.

Lemme get dressed, I grumble.

Grits and bacon on the table with honey, she says as she walks out.

I kept an eye on Lovecraft's box as I got dressed. It still sat in the corner behind the open door. Still shut tight. For the first time I wondered if I was going insane. How much of all this was in my mind? Some of it? All of it? I couldn't actually believe there was... what? A creature in that box? I didn't actually believe that, did I?

No. I didn't believe it. Couldn't. But I had started to wonder. I had started down that road, ayup.

Bobby Jo was waiting for me under the canopy of the willow tree that marked the end of the yard and the beginning of the path to the orchard. I remember it was hot that day, a real scorcher, kind comes only two or three days a year in New England. One of those dog days where even the leaves of the trees give up.

We walk for a while in the quiet. Eventually it's the girl that says something.

Mister Hadley, can I ask you something?

You just did, I says.

Do you have some kind of magic with you?

That kind of startled me a second but I didn't let it show. What do you mean? I ask.

Ever since you come here I've had the strangest dreams.

What sort of dreams?

Strange ones, she says. Dreams like I don't know if they're dreams when I'm dreaming. Dreams that might be memories I forgot, you know? Like memories of when I was a baby. And they're not all good. In fact most of them are pretty sad.

Are you dreaming about the penguins again? She smiled.

No. I like the penguin dream, she says. I been dreaming of my daddy and how we lost him to Folsom and the things he did to get there and how Landry come to live with us. I don't like dreaming bout all that. Or remembering those things.

I think on that a moment and then I tell her, My mother used to say you should think of something happy when you're falling asleep and it will follow you. Maybe you should try that.

Suppose I don't have much happy thoughts, Mr. Hadley, says Bobby Jo and then she goes quiet again and we go about setting up the ladders we'd placed under a tarp the day before.

It's probably two or three hours later we hear the screams.

At first I think some big barn cat is in heat, calling out to her Tom across the yard. It starts out soft and then goes wild, high-pitched. And in that building scream I hear pain, pain like it was a color I seen in the air around the sound and then I knew it was human.

Mama, says Bobby Jo and she's off the ladder and running before I can stop her. I run after the girl but she's fast on those barefoot kid feet.

My first thought is that the thing in the box is eating her mama and in that moment I knew I finally believed. Only it was too late. My faith had come too late and I'd left the creature inside to feast upon the woman while I denied its existence and picked apples in the orchard.

But then I see Landry stagger out the kitchen screen door jug of cider in hand and I understand. It's not my monster what hurt her. It was hers.

He doesn't say nothin to us as we pass on the lawn. Doesn't even look me in the eyes. Just keeps his head down and lumbers toward the ciderhouse.

Bobby Jo is there first and I'm there a moment after. Lynne is on the kitchen floor, back up against the harvest-yellow cabinets. She cradles her right wrist which is twisted ninety degrees from true, the kind of break I'd seen too many of in the few years I'd been a beat cop busting wife beaters.

The girl buries her face in the crook of her mother's neck. The woman takes her the best she can but her eyes betray the pain she's feeling and although she's stopped screaming she can't stop moaning.

Aspirin? I ask.

Lynne nods toward a cupboard above the sink. I go to it and behind a tin of baking powder I find a dark brown bottle with one of those lids that come with the glass droppers. Kind they used to make for real medicine before everything was off limits to everyone 'cept doctors. Morphine. She was lucky someone kept it. Though maybe it was less about luck than preparation.

I take off my shirt and flip it round into a makeshift sling like we'd learned to do in Basic. Hell, I'd learned it in scouts first. I put her arm into it, held it up against her.

Your shoulder, says Bobby Jo.

I thought she was still talking about her mother until she points at me. I look to it and was surprised to find the red rivers of a growing infection trailing away from where Gallucci had put a hole through me. Shoshanna had dressed it good but the infection had snuck in anyways.

There's no time to think about it so I push it away and focus on the woman.

Once I get the sling tied tight I suck up some of the dark stuff in the glass dropper using the end of a finger to create a vacuum. Two drops on the tip of her tongue. She swallows it without a grimace, with the grace of the well-rehearsed.

I'm fine, she says.

Not yet, I tell her. I have to set it if you don't want to go to the hospital.

No.

You want to use this hand again?

For a moment Lynne doesn't say nothin. I can tell she's thinking it through. Of course she doesn't want to use it again, her eyes tell me. She doesn't want to do nothin again. What she wants is peace and there's but one place for true peace some people believe and that's on the other side. Except she has Bobby Jo and after some self pity she remembers this. She was a good mother. And so she nods at me.

Wooden spoon, she says to Bobby Jo and the girl fetches it from a drawer. When she comes back Lynne places it in her mouth and bites down. Then she holds her broken wrist out to me.

You know what you're doing? she asks between her gritted teeth.

Done it before, I says.

I feel around her thin wrist and find the breaks. Two of em. Before she has time to think on it I twist her wrist against itself. It crunches back into place. Lynne bites hard against the handle of the wooden spoon and then faints away.

She'll be all right, I says to Bobby Jo. She's just sleepin. Help me get her to the couch.

◆ ◆ ◆

Landry stayed away from the house that night but I knew my time at Gorman Farm had come to an end. He would sober up soon and when he returned he'd want me gone. Guy like that can feel fine twisting a woman's arm but he doesn't want another man knowing it.

The next day was Sunday and Bobby Jo lit out early to set up the table at the crossroads where she would sell their cider to folk as they come back from church. She loaded twelve jugs and twenty mason jars of the hard stuff into a Radio Flyer and I watched her till she disappeared at the end of the drive before I went to Lynne.

I'm leavin today, I says.

She was sitting on the couch where she'd slept all night chewing on some biscuits and listening to the weather reports on the radio which promised another unpleasantly hot day. Her left hand was swollen like a fresh sausage but it would be better soon if she kept it in the sling I'd made for her.

She doesn't say nothin and so I says to her, You should find your way out to the road today. Should be a good day to sell some cider.

Lynne looks to me and she sees what's in my eyes and what I have planned for Landry even if she doesn't know the how of it.

You don't owe us nothin, she says.

Seen it before, I tell her. It's you or him in the end and if it's you then Bobby Jo is with him alone and that means a whole different sort of trouble doesn't it?

Yes, she says.

And I take it you don't have someplace you can disappear with the girl.

No.

Then there it is.

She gets up then and starts for the door. But she turns back to me, a question in her eyes. My daughter thinks you brought dreams with you, she says.

And you?

I knew from the second I saw you you didn't bring anything more than nightmares. There's some dark on you like a raincloud and if you're not careful it'll cover you up.

And with that Lynne left and I never did see her again.

About an hour after his old lady had gone Landry come back from the cider house limping like the booze had eaten the last of his nerves. As he stepped onto the porch I come out of the house dragging Lovecraft's box after me like it held something heavy.

You leavin? he asks.

Have to run into town, settle a debt, I tell him. Can't take this with me. You mind stashin it somewhere out of the way for a night? Someplace safe?

What's in it?

Nothin, I says. But I said it in a way that he would know that was the farthest thing from the truth.

I can lock it up in the cider shed, he offers.

I let him pick up the other end of the box and when he lifts it I feel something inside shift again and now it feels heavier than it should. We lug it to the shed and he lets me alone with it a moment. I push the ironwood chest near the masher and then I carefully place a crisp twenty-dollar bill from the German's attaché case under the bottom of it so that half of the bill sticks out. Enough bait to set the hook.

When I come out Landry makes a show of securing the padlock on the outside of the clapboard building and then he pockets the key.

I'll be back tomorrow evening, I tell him.

Landry just nods.

In the VW bug, now, I wave to him as I pull away. Even before I'm out of eyeshot I see him shuffling back toward the cider house in my rearview. Not all wifebeaters are stupid but damn most of them are.

63

I drive a quarter mile east on the dirt road away from the farm and the crossroads where Lynne and Bobby Jo would be sitting under the sun with no umbrella and then I park on the shoulder and walk across a field of alfalfa back toward the Gorman place.

Landry didn't scream much. Just a second or two. A guttural bark of surprise that was abruptly cut off.

I'm still about a football field away when I hear it. The sound is followed by a heavy crash of machinery and I watch the shed shake as something crashes around inside. Then things get quiet again and the birdsong comes back, skylarks in the border trees. I hunker down on a mound of earth where a farmer's plow had furrowed the ground and I watch the cider shed for a spell.

After about a half an hour when I was sure it was over I walk to the door and look inside.

The dirt floor is black with blood. Gore drips from the ceiling and runs off the metal doodads of the masher like drops of paint. It smells just awful. A dark smell of copper blood and whatever junk had clogged up Landry's bowels for going on forty years. His body has been ripped in half at the waist. Hips and legs still in his old jeans. His top half is on the cider press. A hole the size of a baseball looks into his skull which of course is empty. Mostly.

A pair of clawed paw prints leads from the torso back to the ironwood chest which is closed and locked again. I listen closely. It's purring again. Was there gratitude in that sound? I hoped so. And I hoped the purring meant that it was going to sleep again.

Quickly and with care to avoid the blood, I lift Landry's body onto the pitted steel beneath the great steam masher. The M.D. would no doubt notice the missing brain but I counted on him to pay that no nevermind, chalking it up to scavengers that had come by before anyone knew Landry was dead.

I walked back to the car then. Then I drove back to the homestead and wrote a hasty note to Lynne that I placed in the center of the kitchen table under a grimy plastic salt shaker. I put three hundred dollars under the pepper.

Landry is under the masher.
Tell them he got drunk and slipped.
Take your daughter someplace nicer.
Burn this.

I got the chest and strapped it in behind my seat.

When I drove out of town I took the other way so I wouldn't have to see that girl's face again.

I had my shoulder to consider, now. The flames licking out from the infected bullet hole were reaching toward my chest and soon I would be good and fucked. But before I tended to my body I needed to do something for my piece of mind, whatever was left of that. I stopped at a pharmacy in Holyoke got some aspirin and a chocolate phosphate and parked myself in a sit-down phone booth at the back of the diner. This time I paid for the call myself.

What the Christ is this thing? I ask soon as the kid is on the line.

You've seen it? she asks and I can hear the excitement in her voice.

Seen more of it than I want to but less than some other unlucky folk. I told her what I heard in my room that night and how, afterwards, I was compelled to write out my memories on paper.

So it is real, she says.

Real as fuck.

What happened to your other buyer?

He was an appetizer.

You have to bring Calliope to me, the kid says.

I oughtta chain it up and dump it in the drink is what I oughtta do.

You can't kill her, she says.

Says who?

You throw her in a lake or the ocean and she will call out to some idiot fisherman to bring her up, she explains. You're still alive. She's bonded to you. Don't you feel her in your mind?

65

Of course I did, didn't I? Ever since I'd walked out of Professor Antone's house with the chest I'd felt her – it – in my mind. The dreams of my mother. Long ignored memories gathering volume, like streams in a rising flood, kind you don't notice till you're knee-deep in the murk it happens so slow.

What is she? I ask the girl.

A muse.

A muse? A muse. A muse means an inspiration. Dumbo's magic feather and all that. But that's not what you mean...

No. That's not what I mean, she says.

What do you mean when you say, *Muse*?

It's a god, Mr. Hadley. A little god.

What she described then was not really a god as I understand gods to be but close enough for government business I guess.

A muse, the kid tells me, is something out of a legend from Ancient Greece. Apparently long before the man Jesus and the saints and everything people in Greece believed in a bunch of gods sitting on Mount Olympus who dealt justice to humanity below. The Boss God was Zeus, who I'd heard of before. The guy with the lightning bolt? What I didn't know was that Zeus had a bunch of daughters. Nine of his girls were the Muses. Or maybe it was three. Nine or three. The stories changed over time and nobody could be too sure. Anyway it was three or nine and they were goddesses that gave knowledge to humans. What they did was they sang to certain men and whispered in their ears when they slept, gifting special people with the knowledge of the immortals. Those special people became the first artists. Painters. Writers. Musicians. The word "music" meaning "the art of the muses."

This kid believed Lovecraft kept a muse in his ironwood chest and that this particular muse was named Calliope. Now Calliope was the goddess in charge of inspiring epic poetry on Earth. Greek myth has it that it was Calliope who whispered in the ear of Homer and inspired him to write the very first novels, *The Iliad* and *The Odyssey*.

It was Edgar Allan Poe, the kid believed, who'd somehow captured this little god. The muse gave Poe the idea for his only novel and then Poe freaked the fuck out and tried to get rid of Calliope in Antarctica, the only place he thought she could be safely hidden. But Lovecraft was a crazy fool and so he went in search of her. He brought Calliope back. Ever since he died she'd been locked inside his ironwood chest.

It was all bullshit to me. I didn't believe a word of it.

Whatever was inside that box was a monster. And monsters are not gods.

But the question remained: could I still deliver a monster to this girl's doorstep when every part of me knew I should not?

If I drive this thing to your house it will eat you and your mom and your sister, I says. Have you thought about that?

You ever heard of a book called the *Necronomicon?* the kid says.

The satanic Bible, I tell her, remembering what Gil had told me about that secret book Lovecraft mentioned in many of his stories.

That's what some people think it is. Anyway, Lovecraft read it so I read it, too. And there's instructions in there. Guidelines for how to manage a muse.

Go on.

Everything has to eat, right? Even these little gods, these muses. They feed on dreams, on memory. Like vampires in a way you know? They eat memory, digest it and then...

And then?

The kid coughs. And then, pardon my French, they shit it out, she says. They shit it out through your mind and it comes out as story. It's a symbiosis. She's a parasite.

My arms tingled as if they were asleep that feeling of electricity under the skin. My mind was fuzzy stuffed with cotton swabs. This was crazy talk. Right? Had to be. And yet.

And yet...

I look over to the entrance of the mom and pop drug store expecting to see the wrinkled, spotted monster that lived within Lovecraft's box smash through the display window and make haste for the pharmacist's brain.

Whether the monster was a muse or a vampire or some radioactive mutant telepathic retard gone insane from living in a box, in the end it didn't matter. It was a problem that begged a solution. And here this kid was offering me an easy way out. Who was I to deny her happiness?

My memories are the stuff that makes good story, she says. I have enough drama in my past that I can parcel the memories out to the muse in pieces over decades before I run out. Before it gets hungry for anything more. My dad leaving you know about. But I watched a friend of mine get hit by a car when I was five. I've seen things. The things we do to each other. I suppose you've had your own dark experiences. She thinks you have delicious memories. Otherwise you'd be dead. Poe. Lovecraft. They wrote dark stories because they had dark memories. This thing. It's hungry for the darkest memories. The sweet meat. As long as you can feed her, she will keep shitting out stories through your writing. When the stories dry up and start falling out of your pen like dehydrated turds, that's when you need to worry. Hopefully you have enough bad memories floating around inside your head to get her to me before it's too late.

Can't never remember what I did next all this happened so long ago. Was it the stuff with my sister or the two days I spent at Brook Farm? It all kind of gets muddled together in my head. I suppose Brook Farm came first. I think so. Because when I left my sister's I had a plan and at this point I still had no plan. Just a bunch of gringles.

Anyways. The *when* of it isn't so important as much as the *why* and *what* of it all. So let me start at Brook Farm and go from there.

Came across this sign on the side of a dirt road in an empty part of Massachusetts. It was an advertisement for this place called Brook Farm and under it was two shingles. One said *Vacancy*. The other was a red cross on a white background and everyone knows what that means. My shoulder needed some first aide.

I turned up the drive and after bout a mile I come to this clearing and there on the side of a sloping valley was this great big colonial with sandstone walls. Another one of them red crosses hung from the shutters of a window.

There were no other cars around and I wondered if anyone was home. The whole place had a real abandoned feel to it like no one had lived there in a century but then I seen the grass was clipped. By the time I parked my car by this gone-to-gray barn a couple people had come out of the main house and were waiting for me on the stoop.

Hiya, I says when I got near.

It was a man and two women. He wore dark slacks and a dark shirt and had a long skinny beard and wire rim glasses from the eighteen hundreds or something. The women wore what looked like nightgowns till I seen that what they really were was just white dresses. Handmade white dresses that reached all the way to their feet.

Hello friend, the man says.

Thought it was kind of a corny thing to say. But figured he was just a loud Christian.

Saw the sign, I says. I could use some help with my shoulder.

Millie's a nurse, he says, nodding at the lady closer to him. She was in her forties. Haggard. Long face. The other was nineteen with one of those all blank faces that ain't too nice to talk at for long.

I have money, I tell him.

Millie laughs.

What? I ask.

Money is a glamour, the man says. A trick of the light. Meaningless. It's only paper and metal. Do you understand?

Money seems pretty real to me, I says.

Can't take your money, he says. Wouldn't know what to do with it. But we'll fix you up. Mend the vessel and all that.

Ah, I says. This is one of them whatdoyoucallits. Communist campgrounds.

We're not a commune, the man says. We're a family. We're all family. And you are a lost brother.

I knew there was some implicit favor to be returned here if we were transacting without money. I guessed I'd be spending the next day cleaning out their communal chicken coop or weeding their Utopian garden or some shit. But I couldn't go to a hospital.

Suffice it to say I went with them after locking up the VW.

Brook Farm they told me was probably the first actual goddamn commune in the whole United States. That writer Nathaniel Hawthorne set it up and Emerson and Thoreau were there for a spell. It went belly up before they were dead and had just been a farm again for a long time till one of these hippies come across it two years before. I suspect they were squatting but I never looked into it.

Some two-dozen folk lived there. Revolving door type situation for the most part. There was the core group of ten loyal dimwits and then there were the strays like me they'd pick up with the sign on the road and maybe they would stay and maybe they wouldn't.

I thought there was more to it than just a bunch of people farming and fucking together. There were those creepy uniforms to consider and a kind of hinky vibe in the air. But I didn't press it.

The main house was fucking old as fuck and probably hadn't changed any since Thoreau and his buddies were jerking each other off inside. Dusty walnut wainscoting. Muted hand-drawn ivy along the upper sections of the pale yellow walls. There was no electricity whatsoever. House didn't even have outlets. No phone. Fucking forget TV. Wood stove in the kitchen and that's where we went.

Millie takes me to a chair over by a wall of windows. She turns to the young woman and asks her to heat her tools on the stovetop. I figure she meant to sterilize them. Thank you sister Claire, Millie says. The fella, he only stood behind them watchin.

Let's see it, she says to me.

I pull off my shirt and kind of wince as it tugs around the open sore. God it looked awful and it was only getting worse. The bullseye was dark purple going on black.

This is a bullet wound, says Millie.

Yes.

She shakes her head at me. Boston, she says.

Yes.

The evil lives there, she says. Lives in all the bigger cities you know.

Guess that's why they're so fun, I says kind of making a joke but she doesn't laugh.

She turns to the stove and fumbles around with something and when she turns around I expected to see a scalpel or a metal probe or something but all she has is a mug of tea.

Drink this, she says.

What is it?

Salvia divinorum. For the pain.

I take a sip. Bitter, I tell her, though it was more than bitter. Tasted like a goddamn cup of cathodes.

But for the bullet hole I can do nothing for you right now, she says. To heal a wound like that you need to expel the evil what done it first. Heal the spirit to heal the vessel. And for that you have to talk to Mother Moffat.

Is she like your leader? Your queen, priestess, whatever?

There are no separate classes at Brook Farm, says Millie. What makes anybody different from anybody? What makes a woman different from a man?

A sense of geography? I says.

Perception, she replies.

Oh.

Would you like to share a meal with us?

Goddamn why do hippies have to talk so weird? That's what I wanted to know but I didn't say it. My momma she had her hang ups but

71

she taught me to be polite in mixed company. Share a meal? I said that sounded fine as rain.

When can I see Mother Tuffet?

Moffat, sister Claire says, kinda terse.

She'll come home when the work is done.

She working?

Tending her flock, says Millie.

Some time after it got too dark outside to see I heard them coming down the hill from the road, a whole mess of brothers and sisters happy to be done with whatever work they tended to. Excited chit-chatter. Good-natured sound. They all come in then and somehow there was enough room at the table for every last one of them. Everyone was wearing the same hand-me-down cotton clothes, shades of blue and simple white. One by one they introduced themselves but after all the years I only really remember three others: a young man everyone called Wolfa Goofa, his girlfriend Arwen, and of course, Mother Moffat.

Mother Moffat come in last like she was safeguarding a herd. And maybe they believed they didn't recognize any sort of hierarchy at Brook Farm but she was the only one wearing something colorful. You shoulda seen what she was wearing. That dress. Long to the ground. Lavender like an Easter candy egg. It hugged her skin in a way that let you see what was underneath. And that's the moment I decided Brook Farm was a cult because you could see this woman's nipples. Hell you could see her labia if you looked close and every-one else didn't seem to care. Like it was no big deal and it happened every day. Only people who are lost in God can't see a beautiful woman's body.

Without saying anything to me she stands at the end of the table and gives the benediction over bowls of steamed turnips and turnip salad and dishes of wild berries. You ever eaten a turnip, Bill? Fuck me. About all they had was turnips. Taste like dirt and make you fart. Turnips. Goddamn.

Let us be thankful to the great mother who provided for us this food, she says. And for Thanatos who did not kill us today. May he find fit to spare us tomorrow.

And we have a bingo, I think. Maybe I shoulda left then but I figured if this Mother Moffat really could do something about my shoulder better I suffer through some harmless hippy church stuff than risk going to the hospital. Truth be told I was beginning to feel a little indestructible what with my pet Calliope back in the car. Maybe I sympathized with the people of Brook Farm, too. I knew something about believing in the unbelievable by then.

Once everyone started passing around plates Mother Moffat nods at me and steps to the far end of the kitchen. I walk over to her and we had ourselves a little palaver. Her face was round her eyes wide like they could eat you up.

Sister Millie tells me you seek succor, she says.

I don't know about all that, I tell her. Just need someone to patch up my shoulder.

Showed her the wound then and she didn't flinch.

I was a nurse for ten years, says Mother Moffat. Syracuse. Till I got my calling and came down here to reopen Brook Farm.

My lucky day, I says, breathing relief for a change.

Have you purged the evil within your soul Mister Hadley?

Yes, I tell her. I'm bluffing, of course. Ain't no man I ever met could do such a thing. But I figure if everyone else can lie why can't I?

Mother Moffat laughs. You are welcome to stay the night, she says. Millie will set you a place by the fire. In the morning you may come with us. We will speak with Thanatos and if you have purged the darkness you brought from the cities then he can help you. Clean soul, clean body.

Who is Thanatos? I ask.

You will know him tomorrow, she says. She gets quiet for a moment and then says, I sense another question in you.

Course I had a question. You can guess what it was. But I was too much a gentleman and too much a guest to ask anything more of her. Got the feeling it wasn't the time and wouldn't go over well.

You have lustful eyes, sir, she says to me.

I shrug. I'm only a man, I says.

Quite right.

So let me tell you just a bit about this kid Wolfa. Funny dude. Sat next to him in front of the big common room fireplace that night. He was scrawny, dark haired. Smelled money on him even if he didn't have anything to show for it. Smelled the city on him, you know? He was out of place trying hard to fit in. Not doing well with it. His girl Arwen had fallen asleep with her head in his lap and he combed his fingers through her blonde hair while we sat there. Everyone was falling asleep around us. It was like I'd found Peter Pan's Lost Boys or something.

That really your name? I ask him.

Wolfa? Sort of, he says. Wolfa. Wolfa Goofa. Sometimes it's Wolfa Goofa with the green teeth. Don't know why they call me that. I don't say anything because I kind of like it I guess.

Wolfa, he'd come to Brook Farm because he'd fallen in love with Arwen and because they were both on summer break from school and she was going to go with or without him. He was fourteen. She was thirteen. A different time. He was into music. Wanted to be a musician someday but was still having trouble making the guitar sing. Neat kid. Really was.

You ever met this Thantos guy? I ask him, whisper-like.

Thanatos, he says around a wry smile. No. Nobody has. Well except maybe Mother Moffat.

Who is he?

Pretty sure he's really Tom. Tom Hitchen. You know, the guy you met when you got here.

What do you mean?

But Wolfa just sakes his head. It's hard to explain, he says. You'll see tomorrow. It's a joke. This whole thing is a total trip, man.

You're not a disciple of Mother Moffat? I ask.

I followed my girl here. What's your excuse? You coulda just gone to a hospital.

Must've got lost, I says, somewhere down the line.

The boy laughs. Dig it.

He's quiet for a beat and we listen to the pine snapping in the fireplace and the sound of the logs disintegrating in big chunks, shifting about like a troubled man sleeping on an old bed.

You gotta be careful what you do tomorrow, he whispers.

How so?

Well just about everyone else here believes in Mother Moffat. I mean really believes her. And all this end-of-the-world stuff she talks about sometimes. And I think they'd do just about anything to keep believing. So don't you do nothin that changes that. If you want her to fix your shoulder you better go along and get gone.

We marched out an hour after sunrise, after a communal breakfast of eggs and gritty biscuits and homespun sweet butter. Turnips too if you wanted them because fuck why not? Wolfa explained that our destination was a cave on the boundary of the property. The cave was where Mother Moffat held her church. And church was every day. What the cave was, was a salt mine that had been left empty some years ago. In the time of dinosaurs there was a great salt lake or something in the region and what it left behind was a great deposit of salt but most of it was gone by the time I got there.

Tom Hitchen and Millie stayed behind and the rest of us followed the road for a mile passing a single farmhouse but mostly fields of corn ready to harvest. Then Moffat and her team cut north through a field, walking between rows of bright green stalks. We come out in a clearing by a stream which we followed to the abandoned salt mine. A rusted metal claw lay half covered by thistle like something a giant robot lost in a forgotten war. A rusted sign read: Gatlin Mining Co.

The entrance to the cave was a wide rectangle cut into the hill and at the opening each of us took a long wax candle from a bucket there. Mother Moffat lit hers from a struck match and then everyone tilted their wick onto hers as we passed into the tunnel. I followed near the back and grew a little concerned the further we traveled because there were all sorts of tunnels that branched off this main one and it would be easy to get lost in there. I just wanted to get this stupid church service over with so Moffat could patch up my shoulder.

Eventually we come to this kind of chamber maybe a quarter-mile from fresh air. The combined light of thirty candles was enough to illuminate the place all right. I could see they'd brought in wood chairs arranged churchlike in front of a pallet pulpit. On this stage was a screen made of muslin maybe. I took a chair next to Wolfa and sat down.

What's behind there? I whisper to him.

Thanatos, he says with a grin.

The crowd quiets themselves as Mother Moffat walks behind the screen. The outline of her body appears as a shadow on the muslin and like I said before it was a nice outline to look at. She brings her candle to a torch on the wall and then the outline becomes even more easy to see, the lavender dress nothing but an aura around the curves of a naked body.

She returns from behind the screen to address her followers.

The end cometh and that right soon, she says.

We beg mercy from Thanatos, the others chant like a Catholic mass doing their part on a lazy Sunday.

We are love and made of love, says Mother Moffat.

And in the end even love must die, they answer.

But we are sinners no longer.

For Thanatos has eaten our sins.

And now Mother Moffat looks to me.

Wo be the traveler who brings the evil from the cities to infect our tribe, she says. Mister Hadley you must clean your soul to heal your broken body. Have you rejected evil? Have you given Thanatos your sin so that he may consume it?

It seems like I should say something so I just say, Yes.

We shall see, she says and then she walks back behind the screen and becomes a shadow again.

Great Thanatos, we call thee, she says.

I watch as a shape rises from the ground behind the muslin. It's the shadow of a tall man naked as the day he was born, rising like a magic trick for that's what it was and not a good one at that.

Told you, says Wolfa, by my side. Arwen hushes him.

I can't help it. I giggle a little because it was so absurd. We'd done this skit in Boy Scouts when I was a kid. Light behind a muslin screen and making shadows so it looked like we had six arms. Yes. The shadow-man was Tom Hitchen. You bet it was. And ol' Hitchen had been hiding an impressive prick under those uniform slacks. Its shadow was like an elephant's trunk and my giggling stopped short as I watched it grow hard, bobbing to a perverse exclamation point behind the screen.

Mother Moffat let her dress fall off her form.

What the Christ, I whisper to the boy.

I know, says Wolfa.

Great Thanatos, has the evil returned to Brook Farm? she asks.

Then we hear Tom answer in a weird guttural wail. It's the sound Humpbacks make in the ocean or something. Real cheesy kind of made up sound.

What? asks Mother Moffat. She is astonished.

Again, Tom-as-Thanatos cries out.

A little god? says Moffat. Here? He brought it here?

I feel all the air run out of me.

The congregation begins to whisper.

Mister Hadley, says Moffat from behind the screen. What did you bring to Brook Farm? What are you hiding in your car?

I knew then my shoulder was not getting fixed. I don't know what you mean, I says. I'm beginning to sweat, now. It's hot and dank in that salt mine and the air is stagnant and I wonder if there maybe isn't enough oxygen for us all down there.

You do know, she says, loudly. And beside her, Tom howls again, his shadow head tilting back like a wolf calling to the moon. Tell us. What is in the box?

This is ridiculous, I shout. And I've about had enough. I stand up and walk toward the stage.

Wolfa gets up too but Arwen pulls him back into his seat.

You have brought a false idol to our home, Moffat shouts. A demigod unworthy of adoration.

Stop it, I says to her. Stop it. It's what I said to my mother toward the end when her mind got so riddled with that forgetting disease she'd think I was her brother. I didn't know what else to say. Just, stop it. Fucking Stop it. You know better. Deep down you're still human and you know better. So cut it out.

You will destroy everything we have built here, Moffat says. You should never have come, she shouts. We must have the box!

And in anger I reach for the muslin screen. I'll show them, I think. I'll show them it's Tom Hitchen playing pretend, Tom Hitchen who stayed behind so he could come around to a back entrance and pretend to be their God. Yes. I would destroy her religion by revealing her lies. I grab the fabric in my hands and I pull it the fuck down.

But Tom Hitchen wasn't there. Only Mother Moffat in the buff.

I don't know how to explain it. I don't like to think about it. When I do I can't sleep. It's the not knowing that undoes us.

This revelation had the impact I had hoped but for different reasons entirely.

Fucking everyone in that room screamed when faced not with a lie but with a truth. Some part of them had never really believed, I saw. Some part of them all had just been pretending. Perhaps that had been the purpose of the screen the whole time, to conceal enough of the truth so they could think they were pretending. Because now we knew all of us that we were alone in that dark mine with something invisible. Something that was extraordinary.

First thing that happened was the goddamn candles went out. Then it was pitch fucking black. Someone plowed into me, hard, knocking me to the ground. People screamed all around me but none so loud as Moffat herself. Her screams sounded less like fright and more like pain.

All I could make out was a faint sliver of light in the distance. I went to it. Ran to it hands-out bracing for an impact with another human being or the cave wall. I smelled fresh air and the fragrance of wild flowers and I knew I'd found the right path. In a minute the sliver grew to a wide rectangle and soon I was out of the cave. I turned toward the old farmhouse.

Hadley! someone shouts.

It's the boy, Wolfa. He's running after me. Wait up! he shouts. I'm coming!

I let him close the distance but I never stop jogging. We're in the corn when he catches up, running in the row next to mine.

Where's Arwen? I ask.

Don't know don't care, he says. Let's get the fuck out of here, man. We gotsta skip.

Yeah, okay.

We break through the last of the corn stalks a moment later and jog across the road to the farmhouse. I make straight for the VW parked out front. But Wolfa keeps running.

Where you going? I ask.

My guitar, the boy says. Left it inside. Just take a second.

Hurry! I says. I can hear them in the corn.

But when the boy gets to the door it's locked. He pounds loudly against it.

Hey! Open up!

Come on! I shout.

Open up bitch! It's Wolfa Goofa with the green teeth! Let me in!

You can find another guitar! I tell him. Come on if you're coming.

Wolfa hangs his head and comes to the car and climbs into the passenger seat. I pull away from the farm as a dozen disciples shoot out of the corn. Mother Moffat isn't among them. Don't know whatever happened to her anyways but years later I passed by Brook Farm again and wasn't nothing left but empty buildings.

A mile or so down the road the boy noticed the ironwood box in the backseat.

So what's really in the box? he asks.

A god, just like she said.

He laughed and never asked about it again.

We parted ways me and the boy later that afternoon at some rest stop along I-90. Bought him lunch at this bar called the Noisy Oyster and when we were done I bought him his first real drink because it was that kind of day.

He don't look old enough, the bartender says but I give him a look and he reconsiders that amendment.

Cheers, I says, and we clink glasses of low shelf whiskey. To forgetting.

Amen to that, says Wolfa.

He's quiet for a bit and I'm getting ready to scoot when he starts talking about what happened in the mines that morning. Can't get it out of my head, he says. It's like a photograph I keep seeing, how you pulled back the curtain and nothing was there except Moffat.

Like a freeze frame, I says.

He nods. A snapshot image froze without a sound, he says.

The whiskey was getting to him. That was good. I clapped him on the back and got out of my chair and gave him money for the bus that would come to take him back to Boston.

Get on with your music, I tell him.

You get that shoulder taken care of, he says.

Will do. Nice to meet you...

Pete, he says. Just Pete, now.

There are paths in life presented to you like a choice and you are given the time to make up your mind before continuing. And sometimes you can see the fork in the road and feel a harsh hand on your back pushing you down the wrong lane and there ain't nothing you can do about that. This was one of those other times.

I was feverish. And this wasn't the sort of fever you take care of with kiddie medicine. I needed some kind of doctor. But the police were surely looking for me. I check into a hospital and there might be a metal bracelet on my wrist when I wake up. Couldn't risk it.

I could feel the fire radiating from that gunshot wound. It itched like a motherfucker through my shirt. It was going for my heart, tendrils of poison, tentacles of a monster slowly reaching out to snatch my soul away.

I didn't have a choice. I didn't want to put my sister in danger. But I didn't have no choice. She was kin. Obligated. Someone I could trust. And besides, she was a doctor. Or a doctor of sorts. And Janet didn't live far. Amherst. Forty minutes down the highway. It was too perfect.

In the end I decided not to call ahead. Better to ask for forgiveness than permission. That's my motto.

She was patching up a dachshund's ear when I arrived. It was about closing time not that it mattered to Janet – I bet she was there most nights till after ten, combing out the nats on a big tomcat or de-worming a goat. We hadn't spoken much in years but we sent each other Christmas and Birthday cards. Least she did. I tried to keep up. Janet. She was the type of woman when you looked at her you didn't see anything soft. Not to say she wasn't pretty. She was just harsh. Like our mother. Fatless. Wrinkled in the cheeks already. Short hair like a boy. Long fingers. Never a smile. Not for me.

She didn't have no secretary then. It was just her in this wide trailer near the college. The trailer was connected to tin-roof sheds where she kept the strays. She got all the medicine and equipment she needed from the state and she didn't need to put any of the animals down less they had rabies or something. I walked through the lobby doors into the surgical room and found her there.

Mike, she says, her eyebrows furrowed in confusion and annoyance. More confusion than annoyance, God bless her.

Before I have a chance to say anything she kind of susses out what's wrong. Probably by the color of my cheeks and the slump in my shoulder as I step through the door. She knows a wounded animal when she sees one.

You're hurt, she says.

Got shot, I says. Went right through. But I guess it was a dirty bullet or something. It's infected.

I pull down the collar of my shirt and she winces when she sees the red like a setting star across my shoulder.

She finishes with the wiener dog and carries him out to the sheds. I wonder if that's where I'll end up or if she'll invite me back to her home.

Sit, she says, pointing to a metal chair in the corner of the room. I do as instructed while she washes her hands and puts on a pair of blue rubber gloves. I take off my shirt and look down at my gut. I was always skinny when we were kids. Janet wheels a tray over and I see all sorts of scissors and torture-lookin stuff on blue paper.

You should be in a hospital, she says.

I know.

So why aren't you?

You really want to hear it?

Not especially, she says.

She touches the edge of the wound with a probing finger and I watch a thin trickle of puss squish out.

Christ, she whispers. She gets up and walks to the cabinet and when she comes back she has a couple pills the kind you give horses when they're sick and a glass of water.

Keflex, she says. It's an antibiotic. It'll keep you from dying. And this other one's for the pain.

I swallow the pills and the water and wait for the rest.

When she comes back she has a syringe in her hand filled with some yellow tinted stuff.

More medicine? I ask.

This will numb your skin so I can dig out the dead stuff.

I nod.

You still a contract cop? she asks.

Private eye, I correct her.

If you still worked for the state instead of insurance companies and adulterers you wouldn't be in this mess, would you?

Probably not, I says.

Janet stings me with the needle and it hurts for a second and then I feel better like there was pressure in my body and then there wasn't. Or not as much. She sets the syringe down and picks up a scalpel and tweezers.

Why do you do it? she asks. You were a fine cop.

People change, is all I say. It was an old argument.

How's Amanda? I ask so she'll stop asking about me.

She rolls her eyes. Twelve and already a boyfriend even if she doesn't know what it means, really, she says. Kids today. You wouldn't know. But... it's not like it was before. When we were kids.

I wince as a tangle of pain flashes through the numbness as she scrapes out infected flesh. She pours peroxide into the open wound and I listen to it pop and sizzle like rice cereal. Then she dresses it with aloe and gauze and a bandage meant for a Great Dane.

Thank you, I says.

Where you staying? she asks, turning her back to me as she cleans up.

Spotted a motor court on my way in, I tell her.

She sighs. Don't be stupid, Mike, she says. You shouldn't be driving. Not on phenylbutazone. You'll stay with us. There's a day bed in the library.

Russell won't mind?

She shrugs. Mandy will be thrilled, she says. Talk your ear off.

What I was thinking was I didn't want my niece anywhere near Lovecraft's ironwood chest. The thought of it made me nauseous. You got a place I can store some valuables? I ask.

She sighs again and then pulls a slim cigarette from a drawer and lights it without asking me if I'd like one.

It's nothin illegal, I says.

There's a cache in the barn, she says. Russell keeps his Browning out there.

What's ol' Russ need with a Browning? He don't hunt.

He had it in the war, she says.

War? He never left Hawaii.

Stop it, Mike.

Janet lived in a miniature Victorian painted red with white trim about a mile from the university on a narrow plot of land big enough for two saddlebreds, a heifer, a cocker spaniel, and a spotted goat named Mixie who was too old to milk and bit anyone got close enough to try. Her husband, Russell Fry, was an adjuster for the county or some bullshit. He made lots of money for never getting his hands dirty. They'd met in school down Orono right before Pearl Harbor and as soon as he was in the picture she didn't come round no more. Mother was on her way out by then. Checked out and waiting for the valet as it were. It was only another year doing everything myself. Washing shit out of blankets and feeding ma creamed corn. Anyhow they had this girl Mandy and she was a hoot.

For her tenth birthday I'd sent her this portable, candy-apple red Electone and a couple vinyls: Presley; Holly; some Patsy Cline. This record player was the center of much drama in the Fry home, I guess, because soon enough Mandy got her hands on some good shit her father thought was going to turn her into a lesbian. Sam Cooke. Jimmy Reed. Howlin' Wolf. She was upstairs singing *Got me runnin' Got me hidin'*, when we walked in the front door.

Their colored girl was dressed and waiting in the foyer.

Sorry I'm late, says Janet.

Meatloaf cookin', the girl says. Mashed taters on the stovetop. Greens.

Thank you.

The girl nods and scoots out the open door without a goodbye. I give Janet a long look.

Not so liberal outsida Maine? I ask.

The last nanny was white, she says.

Yeah. Irish, I bet.

Janet shakes her head and walks upstairs to corral her daughter.

Their home was godawful neat and tidy like a house you would pay to tour the kind where you can't go in all the rooms because some of them are kept off limits by red velvet ropes. You almost couldn't tell a kid lived there. They had no television in the living room. Just a sofa and a lounger by the window where you could read. A baby grand occupied the corner. There was lace under every goddamn thing. Lamps. Glass dishes full of disgusting hard candy that was probably two years old. Kind of dishes mom used to have.

I sat on the sofa and paged through the *New Yorker* only reading the cartoons that were never funny. Trying to occupy myself. I was nervous for the box sitting in the back of my sister's Cadillac and I was waiting for the first opportunity to go outside and move it to the barn.

In a minute, Mandy come hopping downstairs. I hadn't seen her in three years but she jumped right into my arms like it'd been yesterday. Kids, huh? She was a ragdoll of a girl, all knees and elbows and her hair was that dirty blond like her mom's, clipped above her shoulders in a pretty bob. She smelled like sweat and bubblegum. She'd been dancing to the music upstairs, imagining herself on *Bandstand*.

Careful, Amanda, says Janet. Your uncle hurt his shoulder.

Sorry, she says, sitting next to me on the couch.

Just a scrape, I assure her.

Did you come to visit?

Kind of, I says.

You staying over?

Looks like it.

Yes! she shouts. We can play Yahtzee. I still have it in my closet. And I'm really good now.

Yeah?

Let him get settled in, first, Janet says.

Mandy growls.

We'll all play after supper.

Hey Uncle Mike you ever heard of Muddy Waters? Mandy asks.

Have I ever heard of Muddy Waters? I says. Your mother never tell you about the time I rescued Muddy from those highwaymen down Terribone Parrish?

Here we go, says Janet. But she cracks a smile at my story. Everyone likes a good story.

While Janet and Mandy got dinner set up I took the box to the barn. Door was open – a great big orange orb spider was spinning her nightly web in the crook of the doorframe. Inside, the floor was oak plank ground to mud and the whole place smelled of Heaven, of heather and mint and honeysuckle and petrified horse turds, of grain, of a hundred smells of nature that when they mixed together reminded me of home. Off to the side was a squat room for tack and a desk where Janet kept a ledger for buyin feed. In the floor there was a hinged door. On the door was a clasp and a simple padlock. The key, she'd told me, was kept in a mason jar full of screws that sat on a ledge above the desk.

Once I had it open, I pushed Russell's shotgun further back and then placed Lovecraft's box gently inside. It fit with an inch of room to spare. I was turning to shut the door again when I heard the shifting from within and then a questioning voice in my head.

Pim? it says.

No pim, I whisper. No Tekeli-li.

Pim, it insists.

I just fed you, I says, thinking of Landry.

Then it says something new. It almost sounds German and the saying of it is infused with sizzling anger: *Yog-Sothoth.*

I feel an itch behind my eyes in the dense gray matter of my brain and a muscle in my cheek twitches involuntarily. A memory wells up in my mind's eye, a phantom image drawing itself together in the black ether like one of those Canadian TV stations that sometimes bleed through on the stateside UHF band when the weather gets weird. It's not a good memory. It's the day I pulled Dougie McKagen out of the Kenduskeag. Last case I ever worked for Portland P.D.

No, I say out loud. I try to shut a door on the memory, try to close off my mind. Try to think of nothing. It's a hard thing to do, if you've never tried. Think of nothing. Try it some time. Hard to keep yourself from thinking something. I was sure somehow that if I let it get a good strong hold on that memory I'd find myself under that compulsive spell again, that urge to begin writing and soon I would sit down at the desk right there in the barn and write some dumbshit story that was sort of about the day I pulled Dougie's body out of that river. And what would happen when I was out here so long Janet came to check on me? What if she came when I was under that thing's spell? Under the spell of Calliope or whatever the hell she was, whatever it was? Or what about this? Suppose Janet didn't come out herself. Suppose she sent Mandy?

No, I says. Strong this time. Much more like a command. And I keep from thinking anything for about ten long seconds and then I feel its grip on me weaken.

87

Pim, it says again only this time it sounds like a whimper. A curse from a petulant child.

No pim tonight, I says, setting the door back and snapping the padlock into place. Not tonight.

After Russ come home we all sat around the kitchen table and ate the meatloaf their colored girl had cooked. He spent the whole meal talking about a clambake he needed Janet and Mandy to help with. It was either for the county sheriff or the D.A. don't remember which but Russ had some kind of aspirations then to be a county councilman. Didn't work out for him. Couple years down the road Janet caught him in the back seat of a parked car at the university giving the time to a young woman who was volunteering on his campaign. That was the end of them and he never did amount to anything. Sometimes I wish I'd fed him to Calliope. At least she would have been full and not come to the house that night like she did. Clever bitch.

Russ read the evening paper while me and Janet and Mandy cleaned up the dishes and then we played Yahtzee at the table. It reminded me of being kids and how we used to play rummy on New Years Eve while mom snuck gin in her Seven-Ups. Mandy won the first game and then her momma won the other two. Afterwards Russ and Mandy went to bed and on her way out the girl gave me another big hug. If I'd known it was the last time I'd seen her I would have held it longer. The thing about living, though – you never know when you're never gonna see someone again. Best to assume that's always the case.

Janet comes back down from putting Mandy to bed and then she gets out a bottle of dago red from under the cabinet and two plastic cups. We sit next to each other on the couch. I'm glad we have a moment alone because I'd been stewing over something ever since the Gorman farm.

I think maybe mom hated you because of me, I says when the quiet got a little too loud.

She chuckles and almost chokes on the wine. What are you talking about? she asks.

And so I tell her about the scene Calliope had dug out of my memories. About the time when she was three and I had broken the heirloom peppermint dish and blamed it on her.

Our mother didn't hate me because of that broken dish you dummy, she says. Our mother hated me because I was there. She was a depressive drunk who was only sober between eight and ten in the morning. She hated everybody. Even you. She just didn't hate you to your face.

I didn't say nothin. After all these years... To think of all the time I'd wasted on guilt over that moment. Some people they think a happy ending is a guy on Death Row who after twenty years behind bars is finally released when the cops realize he's innocent. That's not a happy ending. There's nothing more tragic than lost time. That's what I believe. It's the only thing you can't never make up for.

You really felt bad about that all this time? she says and places a hand on one of mine. You may be a hard-headed misogynist who thinks women can't save themselves but you're a real sweetheart, too.

That night I dreamt of Dougie McKagen and the dirty Kenduskeag, bout how the ice broke up and let loose early March that year bringing the boy's body down with it. We'd been looking for him since Halloween. He was eight. A right matchstick of a kid. Maybe eighty pounds. He'd gone trick-or-treating downtown with his older brother and his older brother's friends. Sometime round seven that evening they ditched him to go drink rye down in the Barrens. Figured Dougie could get home himself and why not it was only five blocks. This woulda been nineteen and fifty-five.

JAMES RENNER - MUSE

I had a hunch the kid had been snatched by this fella Ernie Whitescomb who lived above the Five and Dime on Congress. I'd arrested him the year before for pullin a kid down the alley and touching his privates. Dougie could have taken Congress to get home, gone past Whitescomb's place. It wasn't the most direct route, mind you, but since when do young boys take the most direct route home?

Got so sure of it I roughed the fella up a bit one day when the kid was still missing. I took him in the kidneys with a roll of quarters but he didn't know nothin he said and he never broke.

It was the part of the job I hated the most, the not knowing. I could take any crime no matter how terrible, no matter how low. Give me a wife beater, please. Or a looter, lord. A grifter come North from Boston. All that waiting and the not knowing. It rips you apart. The uncertainty. No way to process what's not there. You can't divide by zero, you know.

And then the body come down with the ice and the mud. Trappers found it in a crook of the river up by the cemetery in Bangor. Naked as the day he was born. Skin white as a store mannequin mummified from the cold. He'd been stabbed in the heart. One stab but hard. And deep. So deep the shoulder of the knife, what they call the *quillon*, had left an indentation against his skin that had turned black from lividity. It had been a decorative knife not something used for hunting. And it had left the imprint of a lily flower on either side of the wound.

The chief decided it was a drifter passing through. Come and gone. Up to Montreal to prey on the transients, there, mayhap. Sometimes I even believed it myself.

That night I stayed at my sister's place I dreamt I saw Dougie walking home. Not up Congress but across Forrest and then up Marginal. A cream-colored Fleetmaster pulls up beside him and the kid knows the man in the front seat. And as he goes to get in I kind of realize it's all a dream and do you know how it is sometimes when you know you're dreaming and you try to wake up but its like you're paralyzed or something? That's what happened. The only thing I could do was push out a soft moan and

I hoped that was maybe enough noise to wake up my other senses because I didn't really care to see what came next.

I was sleeping in the library on an old day bed against the yellow wallpaper. The moan became a yelp and then I could move again. I opened my eyes and tried to sit up but something was on my chest, holding me down. Her. *It*. I could only make out its basic size and shape in the darkness. It was as big as a two-year-old kid and weighed maybe fifty pounds. Its thick, gray legs straddled my torso. Its talons dug into my arms. I could see the outline of a bald round head with triangular ears perched high on its dome. It leaned down to me. Its breath smelled like the air around a match that will not light. Calliope leaned toward the place on my forehead where she liked to drill for brains.

Pim, she whispers in the dark.

A flash of light goes off in my head and I see Dougie's face again, his face on that missing poster, one of the thousands I'd put up around Portland and Brewer and Veazie that Winter. She's forcing me back into that memory. Tasting it. Eating it like an aged bit of slimy cheese. I can see her chest expand as her body takes in my memories.

I'm too afraid to fight. Too afraid to do anything. Too afraid to scream.

Tikeli-li, says Calliope.

If I fight her now she'll pierce my skull and take what she needs in gray matter. It isn't what she prefers, no. Somehow I know this. But I also know that when you get hungry enough you'll settle for a McDonald's cheeseburger if it's a mile closer than the steak house.

Take it, I think at her. *Take what you need.*

Immediately I sense her relax. And then it happens. The memory envelops me, swallows me, surrounds me. It's everything. And the memory begins to change. Not much. Little details. Things I wasn't present for and couldn't have known. Calliope is creating a fiction wrapped around the facts to make a more complete story. This is Calliope digesting the truth. Processing it. Removing the pure nutrients. The story it leaves behind is the junk, the garbage we desire for entertainment; the legend that only feels true but really isn't.

A farce, I realize. All stories are a farce. And our lives are nothing but a collection of these stories. That is why the gods look down on us with contempt, the way we look at children who play in their own shit.

Distantly I feel her move off me and I see myself walking around the room as if from outside my own body. Searching. Searching for something to write with before the pressure of the story she left inside me becomes too much. It needs out. Out! Out! It needs to be expelled. Excreted. Before it can poison me. I have to get it out!

Inside a desk by the bookshelf, I find a tube of lipstick and nothing more. *Yes, that will do*, I think. *That will do just fine.*

Thank God I wake up first. I wake up on the floor, curled in a ball. The library is gray with early light. It was around five thirty. In another fifteen minutes Russ and Janet would be getting ready for work.

The wall behind me is covered in a dark mess of words written in my block handwriting. Half the story is written in lipstick. The rest is written in blood. I can feel the spot on my leg I dug into. Must've done it with my pocketknife after the lipstick run out. The knife is beside me.

I read only part of it. Enough to see how crazy it will sound when Janet discovers it. The basics of what I know about Dougie McKagen's search and murder are there. But this short story is different in several important ways. It was a dark, twisted story but also kind of poignant I think. Or it could've been. I don't know. Don't remember much of it anymore. But it was about friendship as much as death. How fleeting childhood is and how becoming an adult is kind of like dying too.

There's no time to do anything about it. In a few minutes my sister will wake and come to check on me. Mandy will be waking, too. They will find this, this craziness I've drawn on their wall that I could not hide and in the ensuing investigation of my sanity there will be no keeping them from the box I've hidden beneath the floor of their barn. Janet will need to know what's in it after seeing this.

It's a hard choice. A terrible choice at that. But what choice really? I have to leave. I have to go right now before it's too late. And that means leaving this shit on the wall. Leaving this crazy story written on the wall in blood and that means leaving Janet forever. You can't apologize for craziness like that. And how can you ever invite that craziness into your home again? Leaving now means I can never come back. But leaving now means they will live without knowing what is inside that box.

It gets a little worse. I had to steal my sister's car. She'd driven me back from the vet clinic. My car was still there, five miles away. Shit rolls downhill and picks up speed as it goes.

Her keys are on the clipper ship hook board by the door. I slip out quietly and run to the barn. In the tack room the door in the floor is wide open. The ironwood chest is inside and the lid is closed again. I pick it up and listen. She purrs inside, so loud it almost sounds like snoring. Calliope was sated. Satisfied.

I lug the box out to Janet's car, shove it behind the passenger's seat where I can keep on eye on it and before I can have second thoughts I pull out of the driveway and shoot off down the road. At the clinic I switch back over to the green Bug and I leave Janet's keys on the Buick's front seat next to five hundred dollars to repair the damage I done to the room.

Didn't hear from my sister again for five years. After she caught Russ cheating she wrote me letters again. Four or five times a year. Updates on her life and Mandy's. But there was never an invitation to come see them again. And I was too embarrassed to write back.

Found a picture of Mandy in the newspaper years later. She come through Brewer with her band. She wrote all their songs and played wicked bass. She'd cut her hair and dyed it pink. Beautiful thing. I didn't go see her but I wonder if she looked for me in the crowd. I hope she did.

I drove numb for a long time. Meandered east along 90 and stopped in Worcester for lunch. Got some caffeine and some food in my system and that's when I finally made up my mind to just kill the thing.

I had been stupid to bring it… her… anywhere near my family. To think how close it had been to Mandy. To Janet. What if Calliope had stopped by their bedrooms for a little of that sweet meat before coming for me? Too close. Stupid to ever think I could control it. Or keep it safely locked away. The girl was stupid, too. No one could control Calliope. How could you control a God? Even a little one like her?

I took the new 495 and somewhere south of Lowell I left the highway. I kicked around the back roads till I found a quiet place. Off this stretch of gravel a mile from the main road I come to a dirt track leading into the woods. An old logging trail grown up with nettle and berry bushes unused for a least ten year so I thought. I went in slow to avoid a flat. It was near sunset I remember because the light on the trees was funny. Like too gold or something.

I park the car and then I pull out the ironwood chest and set it on the ground. I check to see if she's still purring. But everything is quiet. Come to think of it I don't remember hearing anything at all. No peepers or birds. No cicadas. Nothin. It was dead quiet.

Next thing, I get my sig out of the glove box and come back around. For a tick I contemplate the audacity of this murder. All that time this thing had been alive if the stories were true. A thousand years maybe more. Everything it had done in the way of inspiring men. All the murder it musta done and how that might have changed history in different ways. I felt its legacy. Its permanence. I was in awe of it. But whatever it was it seemed like everyone agreed on one thing: it wasn't meant for this world.

And now something changes. It's as if the skin of the box shudders or something. Like it ripples, the way the skin on your body does when you're shivering from the cold. Or fright. It doesn't make a sound but suddenly the air is deep with the scent of roses. That springtime honey-musky smell.

It's as if all the plants around us had awakened and were giving off that same bright red smell. That crimson smell. As if I was in a field of red roses stretching across a great hill. Like that scene from *Wizard of Oz* only roses instead of poppies.

It's a warning. I know this on a very basic level like how you know someone is looking at you behind your back. Instinct. This is the base smell of nature sending out a distress call.

And for a second I almost feel like I might know what it is saying and then the meaning is gone and it's just that smell of a thousand roses again. The box stops shivering and settles back.

I draw a bead on the lock. My finger begins to press against the trigger and that's when I hear it: the sound of agitated gravel and then the sound of tires crunching down weeds. Another car is coming down the lane.

I have only enough time to tuck the sidearm into my jeans at the small of my back before I see it. My breath catches in my lungs and I swear I feel my heart stop for a second because this is no random hunter out to check his string of mink traps, no young lovers looking for a safe place to neck, nothing so random as that. It's a cruiser, an old black and white Plymouth Fury with the red dome light on top. Kind of car I used to drive in Portland. A hulking uniformed officer sits behind the wheel and glares at me as he pulls forward and parks the car.

He stares at me. I look back at him. And then he gets out, the cruiser rocking back on its shocks. Formidable. Six-five at least. Broad shoulders. An Irish-gonna-bust-your-skull old-school South-Boston-bred special kind a guy.

Hello, he says.

I say hello back.

His eyes go to the ironwood chest on the ground behind me.

What's going on here? he asks.

Nothing, officer, I says.

I had a feeling, he said, almost dreamily. Driving by, I had this odd feeling. It was like I could smell trouble back here. And here you are. In the middle of nowhere. With a queer box and a look on your face like you're a kid stealin a copy of *Cavalier* from the Five and Dime.

I know this looks hinky, I says.

Hinky, you say? Ayup. Hinky will do. That's a big ten-four, he says.

He pulls a metal flashlight off his belt and points it at me.

Stand against the car, he says.

Wait, I says. Nothin's going on. Nothin illegal.

So you say. Put your hands on the car.

I step to the VW and put my hands on the roof.

The cop shines his flashlight into the cab. It's getting dark fast. He opens the door and reaches inside and pops the trunk which on those stupid cars was actually in the front.

I watch him disappear behind the hood and look inside and of course I know what he's seeing then: the German's satchel spotted with blood and stuffed full of twenty-dollar bills. Very calmly he walks to me then and pats me down. When he finds the sig sauer I feel him tense. He pulls it out of my waistband and tucks it into his own.

Then the cop leans into me, pushing my body against the car. He pulls my arms back and cuffs my wrists tight.

You're way out in the middle of nowhere with a shit ton of cash, a gun, and Black Beard's treasure chest, he says, then whistles a note. Somebody lookin for you, boy. You runnin from someone.

He pulls me toward his cruiser, then, yanking me along by the metal bracelets.

I can explain, I says. But that's a lie. How can I explain? No way. No way can I explain this mess.

He shoves me into the back of the Fury, tucking my head down under the doorframe. And then he closes the door which has no handle on the inside and I watch him through the window, through the wrought-iron grating that keeps me contained in the back.

He kind of stands there a second in the dying light lookin at the box on the ground. Contemplating I don't know what. Maybe whether it really was a chest full of pirate's lost bullion. Then he walks to it and... fuck.

First thing that happens is the box does its shivering thing again like when it smelled like roses only this time it's much more violent. This time it doesn't stop. It shivers, hard. Shudders. And the cop he stops about a foot away from it. He's too scared to do anything about what happens next. Too scared to pull his gun, even. He just stands there, stricken. And then the box peels open right down the top and I realize then it's not a box. Never was. It's not an ironwood chest at all. It's a shell. Calliope is like some kind of fucked up hermit crab or slimy snail or something that carries its home around with it wherever it goes.

She comes out. Scampers out. She's all mottled and wrinkled and grayish, hairless like one of those cats people can get, the fucking ugly kind. Except its head is almost human. Less defined but round like ours. It has no nose, not like people do anyway. Just two slits in the flesh where its nose should be above an oversized mouth with puffy white lips that opens on a double row of twisted razor sharp teeth like a great white's maw. Her eyes are huge and round, giant white cataracts, white as spoiled milk, utterly blind. She looks ancient. Like something that feasted on the blood of dinosaurs.

She crawls fast on her long limbs. Out of the shell onto the ground up the waiting cop's paralyzed legs. She's on his chest in a flash. Her mouth opens wide, contorting out on hingeless jaws. And out of her mouth comes a searching tentacle and at the end of the tentacle where its sucker should be is a perfectly round orifice full or thin, barbed teeth like the end of a tapeworm.

Tekeli-li! the monster screams.

The tentacle pierces the cop's skull above the bridge of his nose. There's a terrible sound like a thonk like the cracking of a coconut. The flesh tube enters, pushing into the hole in an almost seductive way. I watch, helpless, as the she sucks it all in. Bone and blood and brain. The gore expands the cord of flesh as the grey matter is drawn inside the creature like an apple passing through a garden hose in some cartoon. And the sound. That awful sound. Meat through a straw.

I begin to scream.

And then she comes for me.

I'd lost sight of the creature when it crawled off the cop's chest. But then it jumped onto the hood and the Fury rocked on its shocks like it weighed a ton. It pounds its fists upon the windshield. The glass fractures and it rips at the small hole with its talons, making it wider, wide enough to fit through. It is insane with hunger and rage. Rage for me for wanting to kill it. For betraying it, betraying our bond.

No, I scream. No! Get away! Stay away from me!

Its body pours in through the opening like a tumor through a sphincter.

Don't kill me, I whimper. I cry. Don't kill me. Please.

It stands on the seat, just beyond the the metal grate that separates the front of the cruiser from the back and it crinkles its long talons through the square spaces.

Yog-sototh, it says and its voice is feminine. It is female, after all. I sense this, too. On her breath is the horrid stank of her fresh kill.

Calliope, I beg. Please. Don't. Kill. Me.

She didn't do me any favors.

For a long while the creature remained in the front seat considering my cage. Not with her eyes which were blind but with all her other senses which were, I imagine, fine-tuned to make up for her one shortcoming. She sniffed at the grating, ran her lizardly talons across it. When her mouth opened I watched that tentacle creep up and out of her throat, snaking out between its jagged and sharp teeth. The technical word is proboscis – I looked it up.

But I think of it more like an umbilical cord because that's exactly what it looked like all gray and pink and wet. The proboscis squirmed across the linked square holes in the grating and then squeezed through one of them, dancing in the air before my eyes as I backed as far away as I could.

There was nowhere to go. The back seat of the Fury was uncushioned and my arms were still pinned behind my back, my wrists shackled tightly in the dead cop's cuffs. You see in the movies sometimes how criminals can slip a pair of handcuffs under their legs. That might work if you're thin and spry but when you're a deuce and a half there's no getting the works around your fat ass.

That opening at the end of its proboscis made smooching sounds as if it could taste the perspiration on my skin. It was an inch away maybe less.

I'm sorry, I says. I'm sorry. I'm sorry, Calliope. I'm sorry I thought I could kill you. You're in control. You always were. Take it. Take whatever you want. Just don't kill me!

Like a flicked tongue the cord recoils into the creature's maw and disappears. She leans her hairless head against the grate and closes her cataract eyes.

Pim? she asks.

Yes, Pim, I says.

Tikeli-li? she asks.

Yes. Tikeli-li! Whatever you want.

In a flash she's in my head, digging through the rooms of my mind with unleashed desire. She digs. She roots. She violates. She's a burglar in the office of my mind, a rapist of memory pinning my true being against a grimy alley of imagined shadows. She searches for my most treasured remembrances, distant memories I'd tried to bury because they are so awful so dark with regret and guilt. She feeds on these morsels of my life and she holds them up in front of me to degrade me, to make me wallow in the filth I have done as she digests that badness and turns it into the junk that make up human legend, the shit of stories.

She shows me times I've ignored loved ones. Moments when I've ruined someone's day out of spite out of nothing more than simple anger. All the rage. A myriad of memories in uniform. Planting pot on wise-cracking men I've pulled over for a broken taillight. The loves I've wasted by drinking and cheating, by nothing more than simple neglect. Stealing that letter from the boy who'd probably been fondled by my client, Gil Holcomb.

Her intrusion goes deeper. She searches for the beginnings of me. Calliope cares nothing for my discomfort, now. She's rooting, rooting. Eventually she finds it, buried in the farthest recess, a cellar with no light behind a double-latched door. And she finds it anyway. Breaks in.

You know what she found, Bill. You helped put that memory down there. You helped me lock it away in an ironwood box of my own. I helped you with yours. And together we tossed our secret treasure chests off the side of a boat and we watched it sink into the depths of forgetfulness together. Of course that's why I sent these tapes to you and not some other old friend. Not some other lawyer. You have some amends to make as well. You owe a kindness to balance out what we done.

Zushakon! says Calliope when she finds it. She sounds surprised. Pleasantly surprised. The way a parent is surprised the first time they see their child can paint a beautiful sunset – the realization that someone has been hiding a talent.

She makes me watch it, what we did the night we came to Dachau. That young Gestapo who'd stayed behind. He couldn't have been older'n nineteen. His uniform didn't even fit, remember that? I'd buried that memory so deeply but when I was forced to finally recall it I found I could remember everything in great detail as if by sealing it away and never looking at it I had preserved it. I was made to live it again. And you can tell yourself we were blameless coming upon the death camp the way when we did and seeing the skeletal human beings they'd kept behind barbed wire and concrete. The pile of baby bones and empty fabric. What sanity can hold in the face of such horror? So you can say we were blameless for what we done to him but we know better. We knew better then. But we gave into it. Gave into the rage. The very rage that made that war to begin with. The rage we'd just won against. Only to have it devour us the way it did. And we are not blameless because when that young man began to scream none of us stopped what we were doing. Even when he was long and dead we kept taking revenge on his body. It was the desecration that damned us.

Calliope began to purr.

A growing compulsion inside me shuts out my other senses and over-whelms me. The compulsion to translate this act of horror into a story for... for consumption by other human beings. Isn't that it? Isn't that what drives the monster and us and makes us her kindred? We go into the world and gather events, gather experiences, gather information and then we tell others our stories, the stories of our lives so that we can come to some understanding. Eating life and spitting out, shitting out meaning. And in the end is it anything more than shit? Why do we want to share that awfulness? Why make other people feel what we feel? Isn't that a kind of perversion? It is, Bill. It is perverse. We wallow in our own filth and we have this need to pull others into it just so we can look into their eyes and ask, *How does it feel?*

But I didn't have a pen. No pen, no pencil, no notebook with which to scribble out my message in blood. My hands were chained.

And as I come to realize this something new happens. I sense the memories of the creature, herself. Maybe she was presenting it to me, bits of sand through a sifter. I understand then our connection is symbiotic. It isn't just a one-way breach. I can access her mind, too, if only a little. I'm the baby attached to its umbilical cord, the one that is ethereal, the one that links our minds, our souls. We are linked and some of her is coming through to me now. Scraps. Bits of junk in the flotsam. Pictures. Images. Snippets of sound. But she must be selecting it to an extent because what I see then is of great importance to my current situation.

I see a grand amphitheater under the stars, a colossal theater made of granite benches and walkways on the side of a hill and in the valley below

I can see hundreds of mud huts with wide windows glowing with orange oil light. I am on a dais and before me sit dozens of men dressed in burlap and tightly-woven fabric of a kind I don't know the words for. Some wear leather boots wrapped tight to the skin above their calves. Some men wear red hoods that hang low over their faces so that their true features are hidden from view.

And I am in a box. Not any box. THE box. The ironwood chest. Her shell, her skin. I am in the box because I am seeing this from Calliope's point of view because she was there and this is a memory. I am watching through a section of the box that has folded back on itself like the petals of a flower. I am watching a tall man address the audience.

He speaks in a language I've never heard before. A fragmented, slippery language that might have been a grandfather to Latin. And even though I can not understand the words I know what he was saying because Calliope knew what he was saying. The man tells the story of his day, of working in a field gathering barley, of teaching his son how to fish, of watching his wife cook dinner on a spit over a rock fireplace.

This is the way it began so long ago. Calliope says to me in English. *And stories needn't ever be more.*

I start to tell it, then. I tell a long story, an epic of my life, the story of a life the way that man in the vision, ten-thousand years dead, had told his own story to the gathering of men in that granite amphitheatre. It's the story of my life but also it isn't. Things change. Events are altered without apology, swinging on a hinge placed for meaning. The kid. The adult. The war. The job on the force. The disillusionment. The job after the job and then the last job, this job. Except in this story it's you who died in the war, Bill, not that German kid. And in this story I'm not confined in the back of a police cruiser. I am a writer. Not a great writer. Not a well-reviewed writer. A writer of little note and I'm writing this story in a coffee shop in Akron and it has all became very recursive. A story within a story within a story in a room of mirrors until I lose myself.

♦ ♦ ♦

And Calliope will not stop feeding. She sucks the memories out of me like opium through an I.V. drip. I fall into a fever state and my voice grows hoarse from all the talking, all the telling, and soon all I can vocalize are meager grunts and even those grunts are stories. Time loses all meaning. Sometimes it grows lighter and then dark again and I believe an entire day has passed but I can not be sure. Calliope grows fat. She lazes in the front. I can see her pale belly grow distended.

I begin to beg for my life on what might be the third morning in the car. I do not beg with my voice, which is molested from over-use and will never be the same but with my mind. I beg with my mind. I beg Calliope to let me go and when that doesn't work I beg her to kill me

I'm sorry I thought I could kill you, I think at her. *Just please end this. Please let me die.*

My storytelling has devolved to a sign language I made up in my madness. And as my joints begin to seize I plead a final time for death.

I haven't eaten, I think. *I haven't had anything to drink for days. My body is mortal. If you will not kill me I will die anyway. I feel it happening. It's happening fast.*

Calliope climbs up to the metal grate and peers in at me. I'm lying across the back seat, looking up. She fixes me with her eyes and it's the same look Sister Mary Agnes gave me the day she'd swatted my knuckles with a ruler after I'd cheated on a civics test in fifth grade. I'd been punished with pain and we'd come to an understanding.

I heard the car door click open of its own accord and then Calliope licked her lips and curled into a ball on the passenger seat.

Somehow, I found the strength to pull myself from the car. I found the cuff keys on the body of the poor, dumb cop. Soon, we were on the road again. Only this time I felt more like the passenger.

♦ ♦ ♦

Dawn was breaking when I finally got home.

You know what it's like to walk through your front door after a long trip? A trip where you could'a died and you get home and it feels like all that stuff happened to someone else? Right. Course you do. It was like that when I got back to my place in Veazie.

I brought Calliope's box inside and got the satchel out of the trunk and then I collapsed onto my sofa. Didn't have no bed. The other rooms in that ranch house on Flagg Street I used for my business. Files and photographs. Pictures of people doing the nasty in Buck Hill. Just a sofa for sleeping. I was asleep before I could count to ten.

The dreams I had that day were a song of my misadventures. A medley of all the shit I'd seen since leaving Veazie in the first place: Lovecraft's archives, that cube-shaped jellyfish thing floating behind the glass; the German's detached head resting empty on the hotel dresser; Bijou and Cinnamon and her sister, the way the giant's arm slipped into the fryer in the kitchen at Parma; picking apples with Bobby-Jo and listening to her talk of penguins; Mother Moffat and her trick in the salt mines; sitting with my sister as she told me how my mother hated us both. I dreamt of Dougie McKagen. But mostly I dreamt of that memory which Calliope had unearthed from the deepest shithole of my mind: what we done to that young Nazi at Dachau. That was the beginning of it all and why I ain't never felt right with this world. Somebody shoulda told us that one day we'd be old and have to remember these things.

I guess I woke up round four in the afternoon. Took a shower. Put on fresh clothes and then sat at the table in the kitchen to think about my predicament. I had traveled round New England leaving a trail of bodies behind me. This was way before DNA and CSI and all that shit. But if there was a single detective with some grit in any of the several jurisdictions I had committed felonies in over the past couple weeks, that trouble would catch up with me. And I was done running.

All this time I'd been worried about surviving. Now that I was home I had time to consider the rest of my life. And it needed some serious cleaning. But as luck would have it I was a pretty good cleaner. I looked across the room to the ironwood box, the shell where Calliope was resting well fed and I wondered if she might not have room for a little dessert.

Some part of me knew even then that Calliope could be some kind of insurance. That I maybe I could use her to my benefit just once. Got to thinking there was something she could do for me before I took her to the girl, the aspiring young writer who thought she could keep Calliope well fed for decades with parceled-out dark memories. Yes there was something Calliope could do for me. She owed me one favor after everything she'd put me through. One favor was not too much to ask.

Remember Gil Holcomb? I mentioned him long time ago and you probably thought I was wasting time clearin my throat before I got to the business of stealing the box and all. But it was important. Gil was important. Because of what happened next.

I drove the VW Bug out to his colonial in Orono, got there about eight. It was dark and I seen him through the window in his living room watching Danny Thomas on a big black and white, drinking something in a tumbler. I rang the buzzer and he come to the door.

Whacha got there? he asks, looking down at what was in my hands.

I asked you about Lovecraft, remember? Got this outta his archives. Thought you might be interested in crackin it open before I turn it over.

The look that crosses his face then is probably the same look goes over him when he sees a young man on the beach in a tight pair of khaki shorts. Serendipity, man. That's the word. Dig it. He opens the door wide and I lug the box inside.

There's only one light on in the whole house other than the glow of the teevee. It was the kitchen light and it lit up the dining room a bit so I walk over there and set the box down on the table.

Here. Let me turn on some lights, he says.

No. Keep em off.

Why?

Isn't light supposed to be bad for, you know, old documents and stuff, I says.

Yeah.

Well.

Well open it, he says. Gil starts rubbing his hands together like a spazzy kid on Christmas.

Pim, I whisper.

Pim? she says.

Takeli-li, I promise.

Takeli-li!

I place my hands on either side of the box, the shell, the whatever the fuck it really is. I open it. Calliope shoots out like a banshee.

But…

But Gil is quicker.

Something comes over him. I watch it happen like everything is in slow motion or something the way time slips during real scary times. He zigs to the right and brings his left hand up along his side. He's pulled a long knife out of his belt, popping the button as he moves his hand. One fluid motion like a boxer. Thought about it a lot afterwards. And I think I understand what happened. Gil was a predator, you see. More of one than even I suspected. A wolf in a scoutmaster's uniform. Like any predator he was always at the ready, ready to pounce, even if he looked bored on the outside because that's what they're about, predators. Always expecting something because they're always planning something. Fact was Gil was quicker than Calliope and even Calliope was caught off guard.

The knife goes in her naked, piebald chest. Cleanly. The blade is five inches long and it catches Calliope in the air like a shish kabob.

Gil looks at her squirming on the end of his heavy knife for a moment trying to decide if she's a hairless raccoon or badger or something I'd brought from the woods to maul his face off. Then his eyes adjust enough and he sees the monster for what she is. He lets go of the knife. It stays in her. He recoils against the wall not screaming but moaning loud and deep, a caveman like reaction. All instinct. All fear. That's all he ever was anyway.

My heart sinks. A great many things have changed, I realize. My plan is fucked. But I'm not ready to give up. Not yet. Don't think it. I pull my sig and point it at Gil. The gun is cleaned and oiled and full of lead and it can kill him just as sure as the thing from the box. Just a little harder to cover up.

Sit, I says.

Gil raises his hands like I'd said I was going to arrest him.

Sit, I tell him again and this time he does.

I keep the gun on him while I kneel to the floor to see to Calliope. The creature's eyes pivot in her sockets and she looks up at me with something like an apology. But she doesn't make any sound. A dark ooze slips out of the hole in her body around the handle of Gil's knife, still stuck in her.

Why did you bring it here? he asks and his voice had changed. Deeper.

Because nobody would mind if you're dead, I says. And it would do me a world of good if you were. I did some stuff down south that's got to be answered for and buddy you the only one I can think of who deserves to be a patsy.

He tries to shuffle off the chair. Roll onto the floor or something. Maybe he had some weapon in the dark over that way. A lamp or some-thing to bash in my skull. But this time I'm faster. There's a predator in me too. Poor Gil didn't know that. How could he?

There's a monster in us all of course. We're all boxes of skin with a little evil inside. That's the secret. Right? We're all monsters pretending to be asleep.

The bullet pushes through his jaw and out the top of his head taking a quarter of his brain with it. A glob of gray jelly smacks against the wall-paper like the flung booger of a sick giant. THWAP! Gil rolls off the chair, falls to the floor, up-ends the cat's dish of chow and all is quiet in the dark and the smell of gunpowder tickles my nose.

I turned on the lights then.

Another red mess. This time it really is my fault. All of it. I'd tried to fix my fate and made a fuckarow of the whole thing.

Calliope was dead or dying quick. She lay on the dull carpet no bigger than a two-year-old child naked and wrinkled her skin pink from all the eat'n she'd done lately. If she was God she was a mortal God.

Four days ago, I'd intended to kill her. Would have welcomed something like this. But having it happen at the hands of this man and so close to the end. Nothing about it was fair. This felt like a promise broken.

There was more to it. Whatever Calliope was, animal or spiritual, she was unique. At least as unique as unique can be. Didn't I have a responsibility to protect her? To keep her alive? To try to save her? Yes. I did. I thought I did at the time. Back then yes I absolutely believed that. Wisdom only comes with years man. And I don't mean years. I mean decades. It's been a lifetime since 1960.

The first thing I did was lean down and pull out the knife and that's when I saw it. There on her skin to either side of the gaping wound. The impression of a lily. No, not a lily...

I turned the knife in my hands. There on the quillon: a fleur-de-lis.

Goddamn me for not seeing it sooner. The fleur-de-lis was a Boy Scout symbol. And who carried Boy Scout knives? Scoutmasters. All this time I'd thought of Gil as just another funny uncle character. But he'd been more. How many years had he lived free since Dougie McKagen was in the ground? And all this time right under my nose. And I'd helped him.

I place the knife beside Gil's body. Then I put my sig in his right hand, aim it at the ceiling and pull the trigger. A disc of plaster crashes onto the dining room table. To the police it would look like Gil had missed once before eating the final bullet. Many suicides did this kind of thing. Kind of like they get flinchy at the last second. But they usually get it right on the second shot. The powder burns on Gil's fingers would back it up.

I fish around the cabinets in his kitchen till I come up with some scrap paper, a form for a Boy Scout popcorn fundraiser, then I sit down and write out a quick, shaky suicide letter. Kept it simple like mother taught me.

Voices in my head made me do it.

I killed them all. Dougie McKagen. A gay German fellow I met for sex at the Pink Flamingo in Whitman, Mass. Those people in that restaurant down Cambridge, too.

I was going to do it again so I ate some lead.

Sorry.

I could almost hear the litter of cold cases closing behind me.

I put Calliope into the ironwood chest. I cart her out to my car on the street. We make for Mechanic Falls hoping there's still time and that the kid might know what to do.

No no no no no, the girl says. What the hell happened?

Ran into some trouble in Orono, is all I told her.

We were on the stoop outside her mother's place in that gutter of a town. She stood in the doorway behind her daughter, a ghost in a white nightgown her hair in curlers ready for the morning shift at the laundry. It was deep into the night and the air was chill and I remember the sound of the peepers in the swamp surrounding that town because it was almost deafening.

Can you fix this? I ask.

Calliope's limp body lies quiet inside the box and the hue of her skin is pinkish now instead of that piebald gray.

The kid runs her fingers through her dark hair. Shook her head. I dunno, she sighs. I dunno. But then she remembers something and her eyes open wide.

She runs back inside and returns but a moment later with that thick book bound in leather or maybe it was human skin. I'd seen it before. The day she'd sent me on this terrible adventure. And now I knew what it was.

The *Necronomicon*. Devil's Bible. She sits beside the box on the cement stoop and flicks through the pages lit by the gritty light bulb above the door where gipsy moths smacked their heads against the round glass.

Peering over her shoulder I see woodcut images depicting an assortment of grotesque creatures: a man with the head of a goat sitting upon a throne of skulls; a great giant sitting on the bottom of the ocean its face a mess of tentacles; a cat with a ripped ear that was bigger than any cat should be, something called a Beezle. Finally she comes to a new page, a drawing of three beautiful women, the Muses of Ancient Myth. She scans the words below which are gibberish to me and then she grunts in frustration.

Nothing, she says.

Well we need to try something.

The kid continues to flip through the pages of the book. She pauses on a page near the back – an image of an ugly creature the size of a doll made of dripping mud.

What the fuck is that? I ask.

It's a homunculus.

The hairs on the back of my neck stand up. I was never one to believe in black magic or anything like that though a great many cops really do. I was raised Catholic enough to feel the *wrongness* in this picture, in this book, in whatever the kid had in mind. The body is the vessel of the spirit, the way the box is the vessel of Calliope. But nothing in that picture hinted at a higher spirit. Just corruption. Oblivion.

A long time ago, the girl explains, alchemists tried to create artificial life. There are stories of magicians who succeeded in creating tiny, fat humans called the homunculi who would do their bidding. According to legends one way to create a homunculus is to collect the ejaculate of a hanged man and inject it into the egg of a chicken.

What does any of this have to do with helping Calliope? I ask.

Here, said the girl. This is the story of a great magician, some say he was an advisor to King Arthur the Great, you know the round table guy?

And what he did was take the alchemy of creating life and apply it to himself so that he could live forever and never age. No one could kill him. No human, anyway. What this sorcerer did was he covered himself in semen and buried himself under horse shit for three days. On the third day he climbed out imbued with eternal life.

This. Is. Insane, I tell her.

Any more insane than Calliope? Than the things you've seen the last couple weeks? Don't you believe in magic yet?

Hard to argue with that.

So what, then? I ask.

The kid looks at me. Her eyes full of pity and beneath that an unspoken request.

No, I says. Nuh-uh. Fuck no.

Half an hour later we were walking down the road toward her neighbor's farm and I'm holding a cup of my jerk-off juice. We carry the box between us, a hand on the grip. In her other hand the girl carries the book.

This is all kinds of fucked up, kid, I says. There are easier ways to be a writer.

I don't want to be just any writer. I want to be a great writer. Like Lovecraft. Like Poe. To be the best at anything you have to... sacrifice a little.

No offense but I'm the one who sacrificed for this, I says. What the hell did you sacrifice?

My life up to this point has been one long sacrifice, the girl says and the way she says it sounds grown up. And I know she's talking about her father who'd walked away and left her and the family to poverty. And about the friend she'd seen hit by a car as a child. But there was more. She'd been a victim. She'd been a tormentor. I didn't want to know the half of what she'd seen, what she'd done when she felt she was worthless. I didn't crave it like Calliope.

111

There were no street lights this far out and the road was that kind of cheap asphalt that bubbles and stretches in the sun till it oozes into the ditches. You could smell the petrol in it. It made sticky sounds under our shoes but remained firm in the cool of the night. Up ahead a large shadow blotted out the stars – a big barn the kid said was home to dairy cows and chickens and more important, a family of Arabians. When she was younger she had played with the farmer's son. Had played hide-and-go-seek in the barn loft and so she knew about the pile of horse manure the farmer kept behind the barn which got spread out on his pumpkins in September.

This is not going to work, I warn her.

It'll work, she says, because it has to. Even though her life kinda sucked she still had that naïve boundless optimism of any American kid. And what else could we do? Not like we could take Calliope to a vet. She was a little God who lived off human memories and bled black goo. How do you begin to fix a creature like that? Don't you have to resort to some kind of lost magic? Some sort of alchemy?

Now what? I ask when we come round the barn and found the mound of horse shit. It stank of grass and barley and gave off a wall of heat. A lean calico farm kitten comes out of the barn doors to greet us and I push her gently away with my foot.

We set the box down and the kid clicks on her flashlight and flips through the book to the section about the homunculi again. Then she shrugs. I dunno, she says. Even the book's not entirely sure. I guess… I guess you just spread the stuff over the wound and then we bury her. And then wait.

In for a penny and all that. I pull Calliope's body out of the box. Couldn't even tell if she was breathin anymore. I thought not. I set her on the ground a moment and in the sparse light of the stars I go about spreading my seed over her wound. How I did this and kept from throwin up I'll never know. While I worked the kid dug into the manure with her bare hands no easy task itself.

We place Calliope's body in the muck and then the kid covers her up again till you can't see she's in there at all. I feel the goddamn pointlessness of the whole thing what we just done. The ridiculousness of it. It reminds me of this time me and my friend Joshua Myers went swimming with his Irish Setter in the crick behind his house when we were eight. How the dog got heat stroke and we were scared we done something wrong and tried everything we could to get the dumb thing to just wake up again. At least long enough to get back to the house. We set off cherry bombs next to it hoping to kind of scare its heart back on. But dead is dead.

How long do we wait? I ask. We sit on the ground some feet away, listening to the peepers in the bogs.

I dunno, she says. Maybe it won't work at all.

I got her here. I did what you asked me to do. I should still get paid.

I know.

But that wasn't an answer at all was it?

While she waits the kid plays with the kitten, tossing it blades of grass which the thing gnaws on. She takes out her flashlight and gets the kitten to chase the beam around the wall of the barn for a while.

Shut it off, I says after a bit of this. Farmer might see it.

She turns off the flashlight and clicks her tongue against the roof of her mouth, calling the kitten.

The kitten dances away from the barn back over to us and right when it passes the mound of manure, three long tentacles, thin and mealy like the tentacles of an octopus, shoot out and snag it. There was a single *mew* more of a question than a holler and then the kitten is pulled into the shit and disappears.

We jump to our feet. There's this horrid grinding sound and then the shit mound kind of erupts and shoots a stream of cat fur and bones onto us.

Fuck! I says. Don't scream kid. Don't scream.

Somehow she keeps quiet. But she hops around on one foot as she wipes the gunk off. After she settles down we look back to the manure. Calliope burrows out of the shit and rolls onto the grass.

I go to her side but what I see is not promising. Her skin looks grayer somehow and harder. I can't tell where those three tentacles had come from. Scared as shit I reach out and feel her skin and yep it was hard and hardening. Like a shell.

Then all at once Calliope's skin breaks apart and at first I think it's her body that's crumbling. But her body had become a new shell and beneath this is something new. Or maybe something reborn. It's a little Calliope even smaller and more wrinkled than the one I'd carried back from Providence. This one has a barbed clitoris and some kind of vagina so I assume it's also a girl. Had Calliope given birth to a baby girl? Or had she budded off like some plants do, a copy of herself?

You wanna know the nightmare I think about on lonely nights? What if that thing was somehow a part of me? Could part of my seed have been used to bring forth such an abomination?

What the fuck did we do? I ask the kid.

We saved her, the kid says. And when I look to her I'm shocked to see she's smiling and crying a little.

I got the other fifteen hundred dollars a couple weeks later. One day it just showed up in my account. Not even a telegram from the kid. I waited for the newspaper headline about how the girl and her mother and sister had been found murdered in their home but it never came.

In November that year a detective come up from Whitman. Irish fella fresh up from the academy barely old enough to drink. Knocked on my door one night. Scared the bejesus outta me. Thought I was in for the clink.

We found your car, he says. Your el Camino. And he stands there waiting for me to say something.

You did? was all I could manage.

Crushed to a cube in this Quincy junkyard we raided, he says. Mob was using the place to disappear stuff. We shut their whole operation down. That would be Gallucci's gang. Such as it was. I mean he wasn't much of a presence after his nervous breakdown. But we put the final nail in the coffin we did.

My car was found in a junkyard in Massachusetts? I repeated, my heart beating so hard I was sure this cop could see it through my shirt.

In a cube. We traced it back from a partial license plate. Usually they take it off before feeding it to the crusher but seems they rushed that one. What brings me up here Mr. Hadley is a question. Why didn't you ever report the car stolen?

Shit. In the ensuing horror I'd plum forgot. There's always a loose end and here this young cadet had traced it all the way back to me. Smart fella. He'd make a great detective one day. In fact, he was famous for a time because of a case he solved, but that's a story for another day.

I fumbled around for an answer but it was obvious I was grasping for a story wouldn't have a ring of truth to it once it spilled out of my pie hole.

I think I know why you didn't say nothin.

Here we go, I think.

That sexual deviant that killed hisself in Orono. Gil Holcomb? He left behind a note. Claimed to be a serial killer. He was a client of yours wasn't he?

Yes. He was.

He got the drop on you didn't he? Took your car. Went on his spree down our way. You didn't report it cause you was once one of us. A cop. A detective. Woulda been embarrassing. Woulda hurt your business. Even if you do business with that type now you don't want to be associated with them. Officially, I mean.

I sigh. Nod my head. He'd walked himself to an answer, a better one than I could ever have come up with. And why? Because he was still young and in love with his uniform and I was a member of his tribe, capable of momentary lapse in judgment maybe but no criminal.

That's about the sum of it, I says.

He nods and smiles. I thought as much, he says. Woulda saved us some time putting the pieces together if you'd reported it though.

You're right. I'm sorry.

You're lucky the freak didn't kill you too. You're lucky is what I'm saying.

I am. I'm very lucky.

♦ ♦ ♦

The next Spring I opened a pizza shop in Bangor at the top of Union Hill with some of the money the kid and her family had paid me and I named it Gallucci's. Took me a few months of experimenting to get the pizza sauce right. I never thought I'd be a cook or anything but I was done with the private eye stuff and well pizza seemed like an easy enough venture to get my hands around. I did all right. Didn't start making money though till I turned the back half into an ice cream stand. Buddy, one thing we love in Maine: vanilla bean ice cream after a baseball game. Maybe on a piece of hot blueberry pie – which I always keep warm in the oven.

That's where the girl found me again some years later. I was just opening up for the day and she comes walkin up the street. She'd grown up. Last I'd seen her she'd been fourteen. Now she was twenty. Full-on hippy. Bell-bottoms with the goddamn American flag sown into the bottoms. But I recognized her still.

She come walkin over and ordered the first pizza of the day and we shared it in the kitchen and washed it down with orange Ni-Hi's. She'd taken the bus up from Orono where she was going to school. Reason she wanted to see me was to give me a copy of this magazine, *Amazing Mystery Stories* or somesuch. They'd published her first short story. Paid her thirty-five dollars for it.

We didn't talk about Calliope.

She moved to my neck of the woods some time later and came to visit often. She married a teacher and had some knee-biters and she'd bring them down in the summer for Superman ice cream. Every year there'd be more stories. Eventually novels. And then great big fucking novels. Everybody read her stories. You'd know her name. The books got made into movies.

Some of em where god-awful but a couple were really good like the one about the invisible monsters that jump from mouth to mouth living on people's yawns. Always liked that one for a scare on Halloween. Even when she got all famous she still come down for pizza and ice cream some times.

I asked her once why she lived there when she could live anywhere she wanted and you know what she told me? Said it was Calliope's idea. And what she said next I'll never forget and you shouldn't either, Bill. She said one of Calliope's sisters was hiding out in this part of Maine. Calliope wanted to be near her family.

Sold my business to a young woman in 1992 and lived off my savings ever since. I never needed much. Took to fly fishing. Trips to the coast.

Lifelong bachelor, me. I think the prostitutes who learned us in Paris kind of ruined me to anything serious. But I treated each of the women I got to know right and never got on bad terms so that we couldn't get together for a beer years after we were done fucking. I'm a friend. Not a husband.

Still there were times I wished I wasn't alone. Usually the days I got bad news and had nobody to share it with like the day I got a letter and in that letter was a folded up piece of newsprint that was my sister's obituary. She died after a stroke in 1997. I went out to visit her gravesite. Left some carnations propped against her stone. They looked outta place in the cemetery. But I had reason to steer clear of lilies and roses.

And I was alone when I got the news the girl was maybe gonna die.

It was a suspicious accident the way it happened and I suspected Calliope right away. Way it happened was the girl and when I say girl I mean the writer because she hadn't been a girl for many years even though she'll always be the girl to me, the girl was riding her bike in the park and she got caught in a torrential rain and during the storm a three-hundred-year-old tree came down on top of her. Heard it on the evening news. The anchor talked tragic like it was the end.

We had never talked about it when she come to the pizza shop but I'd always wondered in the back of my head what might happen if she ran out of bad memories to feed to Calliope. I mean she wrote so fast. So many books. Calliope must've grown quite big off them. I pictured a house with one of them wood furnaces that fill a house and make it nice and toasty warm in the Winters but then the owner builds onto the house and so he has to feed the furnace more wood that year to keep it so warm. And eventually he builds onto the house some more because why not and one day he realizes there's not enough wood in the world to keep that little furnace going. You either get a new furnace or you get a new house.

Had Calliope finally had her fill of the girl?

I tried to find her. Called all the area hospitals. But a course everybody was calling the hospitals because she was so goddamn famous by then and so I couldn't get a peep out of no one. Didn't know what to do. Luckily the girl sent for me herself. This was four days after the accident.

Driver come out to the house. Big black fella in a suit. Said the girl wanted me down the hospital right away and so I got in the back of his car not a limo but one of those nicer Cadillacs. When I got to the room the family was around her bed and I thought for a moment she had checked out already. But then her eyes opened a bit and she seen me and she asked her husband and kids to leave us to talk.

Calliope? I ask soon as we were alone.

She nods.

You gotta take her, she says. Get her outta the house before one of my kids find her. Doctors tell me I've died twice since they found me. Still not in the clear. If I die here, they'll find it. If I'm here long enough they'll find it. Please take her. Just until I figure out what to do.

Why me? I ask. You've got money now. You could hire someone else. Hell you could hire someone else to take it back to Antarctica if you wanted.

Two reasons, she says. She needs bad memories and I know you have some of those in stock. And because you and I are responsible for her.

Because of what we did that night in Mechanic Falls. We brought her back. And we shouldn't have. But we did. I did. You did. And nobody else should have to answer for that.

And so the driver took me out to her place in Bangor and I went up to that loft above the garage where she would do most of her writing and inside sitting next to her desk was the ironwood chest.

Pim, she asks the moment I step into the room.

Shhh, I says like a mother shushing her baby. Shh. I'm gonna feed you Calliope. But not here. Wait till I get you home.

And she stayed quiet all the way back to my house and didn't say a word until the driver had left. I set the box down in the kitchen next to my favorite chair.

Pim? she asks.

Yes, I said, sitting down.

Takeli-li?

Yes, yes. Takeli-li.

She begins to purr as she enters my mind and searches about for the hidden memories in the darkest recesses of my soul.

And here we are.

Fuck me.

Here we are.

Thing is, Bill, the kid's rehabilitation is taking longer than either her or I suspected and that's put me in a bit of a pickle.

I run out of bad memories a week ago. I never learned how to parcel it out the way the kid could. It only took us a month to get out all the stuff about Dachau and what happened over there. I wrote so much. Pages and pages. I've filled twenty binders with my short scrawl. Been to the pharmacy so much for paper they gotta be thinking I'm holed up here writing my manifesto. Wrote so much my hand went numb and I couldn't use it to write no more. And then I went back to telling the stories out loud the way I had to do when I was stuck in back of that cruiser.

I come up with what I thought was a really brilliant idea. I started feeding her memories of our trip together. And it worked for a while. I got this tape recorder down at the CVS. Got all these tapes. Figured it would take me forever to tell this story. Except the kid's still too weak to take her back and now the story's over and I'm out of anything new.

Here she comes. Bill. You gotta get this thing. Find a way to get her back to Antarctica or somewhere where nobody is.

Don't let the girl keep her. Eventually she'll kill her or she'll latch on to one of those kids of hers. Steal her back if you have to.

[A sound can be heard at this point of the recording. It's at once both human-like and sort of avian. The voice of a parrot trying to do an impression of a woman's voice.]

TAKELI-LI?

That's it, Calli. I don't have nothin left. I'm all tapped out, baby.

PIM!

No more Pim. No more takeli-li. I'm sorry.

YOG SOTHOTH.

I'm sorry.

[At this point the recording becomes garbled, a cacophony of scraping and shuffling and thumping. The commotion ends in something like a THWAP. What comes next can only be described as sucking, the sound a kid makes when they try to suck up a McDonald's extra thick milkshake.]

[This final tape continues to record for nineteen minutes until it runs out. Aside from some shuffling and isolated birdlike twitters, nothing more can be heard.]

Acknowledgements

MANY thanks to the bureau of detectives at Boston PD and the Suffolk County Sheriff's Department and to the employees of the Clerk's office at Suffolk County Superior Court, for allowing me to access the audio tapes recorded left by Michael Hadley. Special appreciation goes to Samantha Alexander who often brought me coffee during long mornings spent inside her office, dictating Hadley's words.

I would never have discovered the tapes to begin with if not for Amanda Fry, who sent me a series of very personal and heartfelt emails in 2007, explaining the circumstances surrounding her uncle's death and the discovery, years later, of the audio tapes in the office of his war buddy, William Latch. Thank you, Amanda.

William Latch's daughter, Sarah, was invaluable in this endeavor as well. And her support of this project is much appreciated. Hopefully this book will help shed light on the mystery of her father's disappearance.

We can only speculate as to the true identity of the famous author who hired Hadley to track down Lovecraft's ironwood box, in 1960. Many attempts have been made to elicit comment from the person I believe this author to be. To date, neither she nor her family have responded to questions regarding the events of 1960 and 1999. Though it's worth noting that this writer's lawyer was rumored to have taken a hasty voyage to Antarctica aboard a decommissioned Russian warship in 2009. He too has never responded to messages left at his office.

And therefore as a stranger give it welcome.
There are more things in heaven and earth, Horatio,
Than are dreamt of in your philosophy.